Nor

This bo

the last date stamped below.

Most items can be renewed at
http://north-ayrshire.spydus.co.uk; download the
North Ayrshire Libraries App or by telephone.

THE FAMILY AT FARRSHORE

After breaking up with Daniel, archaeologist Cathryn Fenton quite happily travels to Farrshore in Scotland to work on a major dig. In the driving rain, she gives a lift to Canadian Magnus Macaskill, then finds that they both lodge at the same place. The dig goes well, with Magnus filming the proceedings for a Viking series. But trouble looms in Farrshore — starting when Magnus learns that his son Tyler is coming over from Canada to be with his dad . . .

KATE BLACKADDER

THE FAMILY AT FARRSHORE

Complete and Unabridged

LINFORD
Leicester

First published in Great Britain in 2011

First Linford Edition
published 2013

British Library CIP Data

Blackadder, Kate.
  The family at Farrshore. - -
(Linford romance library)
  1. Love stories.
  2. Large type books.
  I. Title II. Series
  823.9'2–dc23

  ISBN 978–1–4448–1502–3

1

Off to Farrshore

Cathryn's hands tightened on the steering wheel. She could hardly see through the windscreen although the wipers were working overtime. It had been fine in Lancaster when she left just after lunch, anxious to put the miles between herself and Daniel, but the weather had got steadily worse and the road more narrow.

She'd hoped to get to Farrshore by six but the dashboard clock told her it was almost eight when all of a sudden a figure loomed up at the side of the road, an arm held out.

At home she wouldn't have dreamed of stopping for a stranger, but the May evening was still light, and she couldn't leave someone standing in all this rain. It might be hours before another car passed.

As she came nearer she could see that it was a man, tall and fair-haired. He bent down and wiped the window with his hand and smiled. Just for a moment she was reminded of Daniel and her heart jumped.

She pressed the button to open the window a fraction and leaned over to hear him.

' . . . Farrshore. Could you give me a lift? Cell phone signal . . . '

American?

She opened the door, praying that she wouldn't regret it. He folded himself into the passenger seat and held out his hand.

'Magnus Macaskill.'

'Cathryn Fenton. Goodness, you're wet!'

'I'm soaked! I've never seen such rain. Thank you so much for stopping.' He was struggling out of a thick jumper as he spoke.

Cathryn leaned away to avoid getting jabbed by his elbow.

'Did you say you wanted to get to Farrshore? Do you know how much farther it is? How long will it take?'

He grinned at her.

'At the speed you're doing? Probably until tomorrow morning.'

'We should be in an ark, not a car. And I've never been on this road before. Never been north of Carlisle, in fact,' Cathryn said rather indignantly.

'Well, welcome to Scotland — and its weather. What brings you here?'

She swivelled her head to look at him. He was squeezing water out of his jumper. His long legs, ending in muddy walking boots, were pulled into an uncomfortable position in her small car.

'I'm an archaeologist. I'm joining a team at Farrshore.' Cathryn smiled to herself at the thought of it. 'There's been a discovery there. I can't say any more.'

'Don't worry. My lips are sealed. Your secrets about Roman hoards are safe with me.'

'It's not Roman . . . ' she started to say but Magnus interrupted.

'I'm teasing. Don't think they got as far north as this, did they?'

Cathryn was too tired to give a history lesson.

'Do you live in Farrshore yourself?' she asked.

'I've been staying there the last few days.'

'But what were you doing wandering about in the rain?'

He laughed.

'I started off trying to find a signal on my cell phone. I kept walking — and walking — and then it started to rain — and rain — and then my fairy godmother turned up in her pumpkin coach to rescue me.'

Cathryn had tried to get a signal herself to tell her future landlady that she was running late.

She stole another glance at her passenger.

His eyes were shut. Beads of rain trembled on his hair and on the ends of

4

his lashes. Without opening his eyes, he said, 'Sorry, warm cars always make me sleepy.'

Well, whoever he was and whatever he was doing in Farrshore was none of her business. She was on her way to a fantastic new dig. She thrilled at the thought of being involved in what was possibly going to be a major find.

Plus four months away, to a place almost as far north as you could go on the British mainland, was just what she wanted, just what she needed to avoid bumping into Daniel — and his new girlfriend.

At last they came to a fork in the road and two signs — *Farrshore Lodge* pointing right and *Farrshore 1 mile* up to the left.

With a sigh of relief Cathryn took a hand off the steering wheel and gently shook Magnus's arm.

'We're nearly there.' There was no response.

Just when she thought the road couldn't get any steeper she turned a corner and saw the lights from two straggly rows of cottages — welcome proof that she and her passenger were not the only people left alive on the planet.

Stopping the car, she nudged Magnus again. He moved, but only to re-contort himself into another position.

She gave up, retrieved her handbag from beside his muddy boots and got out of the car.

The Last Homely House

Coastguard Cottage. That was where she was going to be staying according to the e-mail she had received from Professor Gillanders's secretary. With a Mrs MacLeod. The nearest cottage didn't seem to have a name but she decided to ring the bell anyway.

Maybe she had expected, hoped, to see a large, motherly figure, wielding a teapot and a warm welcome, but the woman who stood there wasn't much older than herself, with a long auburn plait over one shoulder.

'Mrs MacLeod?' Cathryn asked falteringly.

'I am. You'll be Miss Fenton? But it's not me, it's Dolly MacLeod you'll be wanting, up across the road there,' she said, pointing.

She didn't volunteer anything further so Cathryn thanked her and turned away. Back on the road, she saw that her passenger was taking her luggage from the back seat of her car.

'Hey!' She ran forward.

'I'll give you a hand with this,' Magnus said. 'Where are you going?'

'Just across here, thank you,' Cathryn said, feeling flustered.

'Dolly's?' He gave a shout of laughter. 'Well, what do you know? That's where I'm staying, too.'

*   *   *

Ten minutes later Cathryn was sitting at the table in a comfortable kitchen being served venison casserole by the landlady of her dreams. She had been shown into a pretty little bedroom upstairs, pointed toward the bathroom and told to come down when she was ready.

'I'm Dolly, mind,' she was told, 'not 'Mrs MacLeod'. That was my daughter-in-law, Sara, you met. And you'll meet my husband in the morning.'

In a motherly fashion Dolly had exclaimed over Magnus's wet clothes.

'I was beginning to think we'd have to send out a search party for you,' Dolly said, retrieving a kitten climbing up the tablecloth. 'Lucky for Magnus you were on the road! He thinks Scotland is small compared with Canada but he'd have had a long walk back if you hadn't stopped.'

'Oh, is he Canadian?' Cathryn was beginning to feel better with every mouthful.

'A good Highland name he's got, though!' Dolly said. 'But I thought probably all you archaeologists knew each other? Oh, that reminds me, your professor came round this afternoon. He said could you be ready tomorrow at eight-thirty.'

'Magnus is an archaeologist?'

'Didn't he tell you?'

'No,' Cathryn said. Why not, she wondered. And why hadn't she heard of him before?

'Now, dear, you look as if you need a good night's sleep; why don't you just pop upstairs? I'll knock on your door in the morning.'

'She's A Honey'

Magnus switched on his phone without much hope that it would work but, to his relief, it lit up.

'Liz? Magnus. Sorry to ring you at home. Couldn't get through before. It was pretty stormy. Everything all right?'

'No problems, Magnus,' his personal assistant replied. 'I've set up a meeting for you next week with that scriptwriter you wanted. And on the thirtieth Chuck Forbes is coming over to talk about sponsorship for the clan gathering film.'

'Frankie got back OK?'

'Yes. Stuck his head round the door about five. We're having a full debrief in the morning.'

'Not a country-boy, our Frankie.' Magnus chuckled. 'I don't believe he'd ever seen a sheep before. E-mail me his report.'

'Is it as beautiful up there as you thought it would be? Live up to your expectations?'

Magnus laughed. He glanced out of his bedroom window where little drops trickled down the glass.

'I'll tell you when it stops raining.'

'But do you think it will all work out?' Liz persisted.

Magnus turned round and caught sight of himself in the mirror. Under the light from Dolly's pink lampshade he could see that his hair was sticking up like horns. His shirt was untucked from his oldest jeans and he hadn't bothered putting on shoes after putting his boots to dry by the radiator.

He sighed happily. How good it felt not to be trussed up in a suit and tie.

'It's a dream come true.' He leaned forward and smiled widely at himself. 'Making a film up at the very north of Scotland. And it gives me a chance to . . .'

He stopped.

'What? Gives you a chance to what?'

'I think my family may have come from round about here. Generations ago, you know. I'm hoping I'll find out. Oh, Liz, talking of family, I haven't heard from my parents. Have they rung the office?'

'No, I haven't heard anything. You gave them Mrs MacLeod's number, didn't you?'

'I'm sure I did. She's probably lost it, knowing Mom.'

'How was your mother the last time you spoke to her?' Liz asked sympathetically.

'Her back's no better. She's in

traction on and off. And Tyler's playing up, I think. She won't say a word against him, but I can tell. It's hard being a dad from a distance.' He raised his eyebrows at his reflection. 'Well, better go. Thanks for holding the fort, Liz.'

'Speak to you soon, Magnus.'

He shut the phone and looked at his watch. Just after ten. The kettle would be on if he knew Dolly, and after only a couple of days he felt he did.

'Your new lodger gone to bed?' he asked his landlady as she poured him a mug of tea.

'Tired out, poor girl. I'll give her an alarm call in the morning. Shall I give you a shout, as well?'

'Yes, please. We'll both be heading out at the same time, I expect.' He leaned forward and picked up a biscuit. 'Would you say she was 'a bonnie lass', Dolly?'

'Very bonnie. How would you say that in Canada?'

'She's a honey. Yes, that's what I

would say.' He changed the subject. 'How's JD tonight?' he enquired.

'Grumpy.' Dolly tried to turn her sigh into a laugh. 'I thought he'd give Cathryn a poor welcome so I sent him off to bed. I hope he'll be brighter in the morning.'

Family Breakfast

In the morning Dolly put a plate of porridge in front of Cathryn.

'Never asked what you wanted for breakfast, dear. Bacon and egg to follow. I can do you a boiled egg if you prefer. I've got my own hens. Did you sleep well? The gulls can be noisy at the back of the house.'

Cathryn smiled at her landlady.

'I usually just buy a cappuccino on my way into work,' she confessed, 'but that smells so good.'

It tasted good, too. She was surprised to find, after a dreamless sleep, that she felt completely refreshed. Maybe it was because the rain had cleared and there was a smell of sea air coming through the open kitchen window.

The back of Coastguard Cottage sloped down to the cliffs; beyond that she could see a strip of white sand and beyond that the blue-grey sea where the waves were dancing all the way to — where? America? One of the Hebridean islands? She would have to check on the map.

Footsteps sounded on the stairs.

'That will be Magnus.' Dolly went to open the door.

Cathryn stopped in the act of putting her fork into a perfect circle of egg yolk as Magnus came forward holding out his hand.

'Cathryn. Thanks again for last night. Look forward to working with you. Lancaster, you're at, isn't it?'

She nodded.

'And yourself?'

Magnus had his back turned to Dolly. He made a little face at Cathryn, raising one eyebrow quirkily and mouthing, 'Later.'

Later. Though she kept her face pleasant, inside she was puzzling over him. All that rubbish about Roman hoards when he was apparently an archaeologist himself!

First Day

'Having a longer walk than I expected last night has given me a ferocious appetite,' Magnus said. 'Cathryn, I think you and I have landed on our feet here.'

As he sat opposite her, Cathryn had an opportunity to see him closer up. In daylight she could see he really didn't look like Daniel at all.

Daniel's face was aquiline, his eyes dark grey. He was never seen wearing anything other than a designer suit and crisp white shirt. He wore his hair swept back and sported a tiny silver stud in one ear.

Evidently Magnus hadn't had time to

shave this morning. Or comb his hair, which was fair with red lights; two pieces actually stuck up like horns. He looked, Cathryn thought, like an illustration of a Viking in a child's book. Though the Vikings never wore horned helmets, it certainly made for dramatic pictures.

'Granny, Granny. Eggs!' A girl of about seven, with two short pigtails tied with green ribbon, burst into the kitchen.

'Eggs, is it, darling? Well, we better go and get them. Listen, though. This is Cathryn come to stay with us for a wee while, same as Magnus. Cathryn, this is Rosie. Say hello, Rosie.'

But Rosie had retreated behind Dolly's skirt and, peeping at Cathryn, refused to say a word.

Dolly put her hand on Rosie's head.

'She'll soon be so chatty, Cathryn, you'll be putting your fingers in your ears. Now, let's go and find these eggs, Rosie Posie.'

Left alone, Cathryn and Magnus

were silent, the only sounds the clink of cutlery and the crunch of the last piece of toast being eaten.

From his side of the table Magnus saw a woman, of probably about twenty-eight, five years younger than himself. Her thick chestnut hair was tied back. Her eyes were golden-brown, wide and clear, but there were dark shadows underneath.

He opened his mouth to speak but she was standing up and carrying her dishes over to the sink. He joined her with his own plate, his footsteps silent on the linoleum since, as Cathryn realised, he was in his stocking feet.

They stood looking out of the window above the sink.

Dolly and Rosie were coming up the path to the back door, Rosie clutching a little basket.

'Great kid, that,' Magnus said. 'Asking all sorts of questions about the Vikings. Look.'

He indicated a cupboard door covered with pictures including one done in bright wax crayons of a Viking longship, the dragon-head breathing fire.

'That's a brilliant picture,' Cathryn said to Rosie as she came in.

Rosie smiled at her briefly then dived down to pick up the stripy kitten.

Cathryn stroked the kitten's tiny ears.

'What's her name?'

'Bee,' Rosie whispered. 'But she's a boy kitten.'

They were all laughing when the kitchen door banged open and in rolled a large man in a wheelchair, wearing a tartan dressing-gown.

'Good morning, good morning.' He smiled around genially. 'You must be Miss Fenton.

'JD's the name.' He held out his hand.

Dolly saw Cathryn's surprise.

'My husband, John Donald. JD for short.'

JD's huge hand folded around Cathryn's for a moment before Rosie rushed over and thrust the kitten at him.

'Grandpa, look after Bee. I can see the bus coming.'

Dolly handed Rosie her jacket and schoolbag.

'You're coming to us after school, remember?'

'Is Mum going to Inverness again?'

'Yes, you know she's doing a course at the college on Wednesdays,' Dolly said.

Magnus pulled gently on one of Rosie's pigtails.

'Hey, Rosie. Don't forget you and I are going to have a walk along the beach sometime to find that cave you were talking about.'

Dolly looked after him with affection as she ushered Rosie out.

'I should have cleaned his boots.'

'Why should you? He's perfectly capable of doing them himself,' Cathryn said, amused.

'It's the way I was brought up, my dear. But maybe you're right. Maybe we shouldn't be running after the men folk. But then, how are things to be done properly if we don't do them?'

She was laughing as she finished clearing the table.

Just before 8.30, Cathryn stepped outside the front door and took a deep breath. Human habitation seemed out of place in these surroundings, she decided. It looked almost too wild a landscape for anyone to settle in. But it was settled and had probably been so since before the Vikings arrived over 1200 years ago.

'Cathryn! Hello!' The professor was striding along the road, impatient to be getting on with things.

He shook her hand in a crushing grip.

'Great to see you. You got my briefing? Good, good. The other two have gone on ahead to the site so we're just waiting for Magnus Macaskill. You'll have met him, of course, since you're both staying with the lovely Dolly?'

'Yes,' Cathryn said, 'but, Professor Gillanders, who is he?'

'Gil, call me Gil. Even my wife calls me Gil.' The professor could be heard halfway to Norway. 'Ah, here's Magnus now.'

They walked back down between the cottages and up a sandy path. At the top the professor stopped and pointed.

'Down there. That's where the ring was found.'

Cathryn remembered the first time she'd heard about it in a confidential letter from Gil. Part of the cliff had become eroded and fallen into the sea. Someone walking along the beach had found a Viking ring of finely plaited gold and some coins, just below the slippage.

Now, a year later, plans were in place for a dig up on the cliff before further erosion might mean the loss of the opportunity to see if there had been a Viking settlement here.

She stood looking out to sea, seeing in her imagination a longboat landing on the beach. Perhaps Magnus was imagining the same scene. Gil put an arm round each of them.

'It's going to be good. I feel it in my old bones. I feel it with my nose.'

United by Gil's arms Cathryn and Magnus smiled at each other. If Gil said so it must be true. It was going to be good.

Meeting The Team

'This is HQ.' Gil waved his hand towards a large caravan.

'Cathryn!' A small round figure in a red beanie hat shot over. Cathryn was delighted to see Thelma Strong, an old acquaintance.

Beside Thelma was lanky, bespectacled Peter Jackson.

Cathryn recognised the name but not the face.

The professor did the introductions.

'Macaskill, Macaskill,' Thelma repeated, looking bluntly at Magnus. 'No, never heard of you. Canadian, you say?'

'Vancouver,' Magnus said, smiling, as

Gil urged them on to 'HQ'.

Cathryn found herself squashed in beside Magnus on one side of the table. Once again he seemed to be having trouble fitting his legs into a small space.

Talking rapidly, and with arm movements that put his table companions in imminent danger, Gil outlined the plan for the day. The area had already been marked off, the turf lifted and the soil sent off for analysis. Now they had the painstaking task of digging and sifting and — hopefully — recording and photographing what they found.

Cathryn was aware of Peter Jackson's friendly eyes on her.

'That was a great paper you gave in Stockholm,' he said. 'I hoped to speak to you afterwards but you'd gone. You didn't stay for the dinner?'

'I was sorry to miss it,' Cathryn replied.

Daniel had flown out and surprised her by appearing in the foyer of the conference centre after she had delivered her paper, and whisked her off to a much more glamorous hotel.

Her first reaction had been one of delight at the gesture but later a part of her couldn't help feeling that dinner with her colleagues would have rounded off what had been a very successful meeting.

Since then it had crossed her mind that maybe it had been Daniel's intention that she miss the dinner and its networking opportunities.

Gil interrupted her memories.

'Thelma, Cathryn, Peter. Now, you've all been very polite to Mr Macaskill but no doubt you're wondering why he's here. Magnus, would you like to explain yourself?'

Like a lion caged up for too long, Magnus sprang out from behind the table. His dishevelled hair touched the caravan roof as he turned to face them.

'Thank you, Gil. Well, ladies, Peter, no, I'm not an archaeologist. To be brief, I'm third-generation Canadian with Scottish roots as my name implies, but the reason I'm here is that I run MM Films. Which you've probably never heard of,' he added.

Three of his audience shook their heads.

Magnus laughed.

'You will! We're hoping, if all goes according to plan, to film this dig and be the first to break the news of what we all hope will be a major find.'

Reluctant Stars

He stopped. If he had been expecting gasps of excitement or approval he was to be disappointed.

Thelma squared her shoulders.

'I hope it doesn't mean that we'll have hordes of people up here trampling over the ground with metal detectors.'

'Of course not,' the professor said soothingly, 'we're keeping it all very low-key at the moment. And it's hardly the easiest place to get to, as you know.'

Magnus was Thelma's next target. She frowned at him.

'I'm certainly not one of those people who want to be famous for fifteen minutes. It's never been my wish to be on TV. A *celebrity*,' she said, putting sarcastic emphasis on the last word.

'We won't ask you to do anything you don't want to do, Thelma,' Magnus replied, his lips twitching. 'Personally, I think you'll come across really well. But I'm not making 'Time Team', you know. The dig here will probably just take up half-an-hour in a six-part series about the Vikings. It's their history that matters but we have to put it over in a way that will engage the public. What do the others think? Peter?'

'My mum will be thrilled,' he said, and they all laughed. 'I think it's great. I mean it's such a fantastic subject; it's got everything — power struggles, sea voyages, treasure. You couldn't make it up.'

'Thank you, Peter, That's just the

attitude I was hoping for. What do you think, Cathryn?' He looked at her, his deep blue eyes challenging.

She said slowly, 'I suppose I agree with both Thelma and Peter. I've never had any wish to be on television but if that's the way it is, well, I hope we find plenty for them to see.'

She couldn't resist adding: 'So when are you going to tell Dolly she's got a hot-shot film director staying with her? She's definitely under the impression that you're an archaeologist.'

Magnus looked slightly embarrassed.

'She assumed I was and I didn't tell her different,' he said. 'I will tell her soon, though. She does know that I'm going to be coming and going, though, not like the rest of you.

'I'll be filming in Orkney and Shetland and down the west coast, too. And in Denmark and Norway. I'd be grateful if you'd keep it all under your hats until we're a bit farther on.'

Thelma touched her woolly hat in mock salute.

'I hope you won't want us to wear *make-up*,' she said, emphasising the last word again.

Magnus smiled at her.

'No-one need wear make-up unless they do already. That includes you, Peter,' he added and even Thelma joined in the outburst of laughter.

Gil jumped up.

'Well, let's get on with it, boys and girls,' he said. 'Let's do what we came here to do.'

Viking Treasure

The air coming off the sea was bracing and Cathryn was glad of her waterproof boots, pink fleece top and quilted body warmer.

Every so often she lifted her head to look across the stunning view from the top of the cliffs. The combination of sun and breeze ruffled up the waves and made the water sparkle. White-edged waves fell gently on to the empty beach.

The salty air reminded her of Cornwall, where she'd been born.

She was aware of Magnus walking round the site making notes, stopping to speak to the others. Now he hunkered down beside her.

'I hope it's not going to worry you, this TV thing, Cathryn,' he said softly. 'It's not a 'Time Team' format but even if it was you'd be great.'

I bet he said exactly the same thing to Thelma and Peter, Cathryn thought.

'I doubt I'll be 'great',' she said, 'but it's certainly an interesting idea.'

'And remember,' Magnus added, 'it could mean a lot to the people round here. Financially, I mean. Bring the tourists in. Not yet, of course,' he added hastily as Cathryn opened her mouth to protest, 'but just picture it maybe in a few years. Excavation open for all to see. Education centre. Viking re-enactments.'

'Re-enacting what exactly?'

Magnus quailed a little under Cathryn's gaze.

'Well, not all the gory details, I suppose,' he said. 'We can hardly have a longboat coming in and wreaking death and destruction.'

'It certainly sounds as if we need that education centre.' Cathryn picked up her trowel again.

Magnus leaned forward.

'Do you know you've got some mud on your nose?'

He leaned further towards her and brushed it off. Close up she could see that his chin had a sprinkling of golden stubble.

She stood up and straightened her back, this time looking down at the settlement that was Farrshore: two rows of cottages with the sea on one side and up on the hill a few houses and a lot of sheep.

She'd have to ask if they got broadband up here. Then at least she could e-mail her friends and see what was happening in the outside world. Her own world.

It seemed very far away.

Dinner At Dolly's

When Cathryn came downstairs after getting back from the site and having a shower, Dolly showed her into the front room, with its stiff furniture and vase of dried flowers in front of the fireplace.

Dolly moved these to one side and set a match to the paper and sticks in the grate.

'Now sit you down,' Dolly said. 'I know what the air up here does to folk who aren't used to it. I'll call you through at seven. I hope you don't mind eating in the kitchen?'

Cathryn assured her that she didn't mind at all and after the older woman had left the room she sat enjoying the fire's warmth and crackle. The magazines beside her chair didn't appeal to her so she went and looked out of the window.

Across the road was the cottage whose occupant she had encountered last night. Dolly's daughter-in-law, Sara.

She was standing in her doorway, talking to Magnus. It was unclear whether Magnus had been inside and was just leaving, or had just arrived.

Now Cathryn stepped back so that she was hidden by the long curtains. Sara had her hand on Magnus's arm and was smiling at him.

As Magnus turned and came across the road to Dolly's cottage Cathryn flew back to her chair and picked up the first thing that came to hand from the magazine rack.

It turned out to be the local newspaper, the 'Northern Star'. Before she had a chance to read it, Dolly called, 'Your supper's ready, my dear.'

She stood in the doorway with Rosie half hiding behind her skirt. Suddenly Rosie rushed to Cathryn.

'That's me!' she shouted, pointing.

Cathryn wasn't very used to children. She peered at the paper.

'Is it?'

'Look!' Rosie stabbed at a picture.

Rosie scores! was the caption. Apparently several Highland primary schools had had a trip to visit Inverness Caley Thistle and were allowed to play on their pitch.

'Well done, Rosie,' Cathryn said, trying to remember anything she might know about football.

'Yes, that's terrific. Your mum was telling me about it.' Magnus's voice suddenly emerged above Dolly's head.

How did Magnus know Rosie's mum, Cathryn wondered. Oh, wait a minute. The penny dropped. Rosie must be Sara's daughter.

Magnus came into the sitting room, picked Rosie up and turned her upside down, much to the little girl's squealing delight. When she was upright she launched herself at Cathryn, her former shyness gone.

'Did you find the treasure, Cathryn?'

'Not yet, Rosie.' Cathryn tried to explain. 'It can take months, even years. The Vikings were here a long time ago, so any treasures will be buried very deep.'

'My daddy said there would be gold and jewels. Can I come and see?' Rosie jumped towards Magnus who lifted her up again.

'There's nothing to see yet. When we find treasure I promise I'll show you. OK?'

'Rosie's missing her daddy, aren't you, pet.' Dolly turned to Cathryn. 'Joe's on the oil rigs, two weeks on, two weeks off. Away home now, Rosie, pet.'

★   ★   ★

The kitchen table was laid for two.

'What about yourself and JD?' Magnus asked Dolly as she put fried trout, new potatoes and peas in front of them.

'We've eaten. JD's gone to bed. He gets tired so easily. We had a bit of excitement earlier. Did you see that big house through the trees, before you turn up the hill? Farrshore Lodge. It's been empty for a year but now an actor's bought it, Sara heard — the one who played the baddie in that soap. Ooh, what's his name? I can't remember. It's certainly all go in Farrshore these days. Now, I'm away to shut the hens in.'

'What happened to JD, do you know?' Cathryn asked in a low voice as the back door shut behind Dolly.

'Some accident at sea a year ago — when he was out on a lifeboat rescue. Made up his mind he'll never walk or work again, Sara says. Gets these black-dog moods sometimes. But when he's on form he's got some great stories.'

'Poor Dolly. That must make life hard for her. Is that why she has to take in lodgers?'

Before Magnus could reply Dolly came back, and when they had finished their main course followed by apricot crumble, she insisted that they have their coffee back in the sitting room.

Cathryn and Magnus sat, as stiffly as the furniture, in an armchair on each side of the fireplace.

Magnus picked up the paper and flicked through it.

'Ever done any Scottish dancing, Cathryn?' he asked.

'Pardon?'

'Scottish dancing. You know, at a ceilidh? They're great!' Magnus went on. 'I've been to some put on by Highland societies in Canada, believe it or not. You don't have to know complicated steps, you just try and follow everyone else.'

Magnus shook the paper.

'I've just seen here that there's going to be a ceilidh in Strathbuie next month. That's a few miles across country from here. I'll mention it to Gil — staff outing and all that.'

Cathryn suddenly felt more tired than she ever remembered feeling in her life. Dolly was obviously right about the air up here.

She stood up.

Suddenly there was a long leg stretched out, barring her way.

'Hey, lighten up, Cathryn. We're all in this together for the next few months. We could have some fun along the way. What's wrong with going to a dance?'

Because dancing is what I do, did, with Daniel, she thought.

'I didn't come here to dance.'

I sound like Thelma, she realised.

'I've never done any Scottish dancing,' she said in a slightly softer tone.

'Well, so what? You'll never be younger to learn, as my old dad always tells me. Where are you off to?'

'I'm going upstairs.' Cathryn put her hand to her mouth to hide a yawn.

Magnus left his leg stretched out for a moment before he withdrew it, allowing her to pass.

'Sweet dreams, Cathryn,' he said.

* * *

Looking out of her window, out to sea, she had that feeling again of being marooned, of being the only person left in the world.

Her bedroom was cooler than the sitting room where the warmth of the fire had made her eyelids droop. Up here she felt wide awake again. It wasn't even nine o'clock, after all.

Suddenly she longed to speak to someone from her own life. Her laptop looked alien in this room with its sloping ceiling and flowered wallpaper.

A minute later she was delighted to find that she had two e-mail messages.

First, one from Mum and Dad, hoping she'd arrived safely. She fired off a quick reply, letting them know she'd write at more length later.

The second was from Lucy, her best friend in Lancaster.

Hey, Braveheart, how're you doing up there? Any Highland lairds you want some help with? Guess what? The rumour is that Daniel's latest has been seen WITH SOMEONE ELSE. What do you think of that? I've just Googled Farrshore — looks like you're falling off the end of the universe. Please confirm you're OK! Can you text? Do they have electricity?? Love, Luce X

It did Cathryn good just to see Lucy's name in black and white. She felt a little bit less like Alice down the rabbit hole, away from every familiar thing.

She e-mailed back quickly.

Great to hear from you. It's beautiful here and the natives are friendly! Don't want to hear about Daniel — the only men I'm interested in have been dead for over 1000 years! Mobile signal not good. Will e-mail you again soon. Miss you. C.

Feeling happier, she thought over what Lucy had said. Daniel's girlfriend with someone else? Well, it didn't mean anything. She was probably with a colleague. Her brother? Her cousin?

Cathryn looked back at herself and smiled ruefully.

Daniel was history and the more she came to terms with that the happier she would be. A few weeks here and she'd forget he ever existed.

She deliberately focused her mind on work.

She would love to see that ring, the

plaited gold ring. Had it been given by a man to a woman, long, long ago? Viking men wore rings, too, she knew. Maybe when she saw it, maybe even tried it on herself, she might know, might get some feeling for the person it had belonged to. Did it have the same significance that a ring might have in the twenty-first century? To have and to hold . . .

Downstairs in the hall the telephone was ringing. She heard Dolly answer it and then call for Magnus.

'It's your father, my dear, on the phone from Canada.'

Cathryn saw the top of Magnus's head as he came out into the hall.

'Dad? Good to hear you.'

Not wanting to eavesdrop, Cathryn went into her room and shut the door.

News From Home

Magnus was down to breakfast before her, sitting with his porridge bowl in front of him.

As usual, Rosie had run in to say hello to Bee and was sitting with him on her knee.

'Tyler's a funny name,' she was saying. 'How old is he?'

'He's ten,' Magnus said. 'Do you think it will be all right for him to go to school with you? Would you like that?'

'Speaking of school,' Dolly said, 'I can hear the bus coming. Quick, get your bag.'

Rosie lingered for a last cuddle.

'Can he play football? I'll teach him if he can't.'

'Basketball's his game,' Magnus said.

Cathryn helped herself to porridge while Dolly was saying goodbye to Rosie.

Magnus was pale, and even more unshaven than usual.

He put his hand to his mouth and yawned.

'Sorry, didn't sleep too well. Had a bit of a shock last night.'

He stirred his porridge round and round.

'It's my mom. She's had a back problem for years and the doctors have decided that they need to operate. She and my dad have been taking care of my son, Tyler.'

He stopped and poured milk into his bowl.

'Well, Tyler's a bit of a handful and Dad's not as young as he was. He doesn't think he can cope with him on his own. So he's sending him over to spend the summer with me.'

2

Predicament

'What do you think you'll do about your son?' Cathryn asked Magnus, as she and the team put down some tarpaulins on the damp grass to sit on at lunchtime.

'I suppose I'll have to base myself in London, get a childminder to look after Tyler when I can't have him with me. But for two months . . . ' He poured some coffee from his flask. 'I just don't know.'

Peter gave a grimace when he saw the vast pile of corned beef sandwiches his landlady had provided, and tried to persuade Cathryn to swap them for Dolly's cheese and chutney rolls.

'I'm sorry, Peter, but I'm not keen on corned beef either.' She took pity on him. 'You can have my bag of crisps, and maybe Magnus will donate his fruitcake.'

'I might,' Magnus said, 'in return for company when I drive down to Inverness on Saturday.'

'Sounds like a fair exchange,' Peter agreed, leaning over for the chunk of home-made cake.

'Cathryn, Thelma — are you coming?' Magnus looked round. 'I'm going into the museum to talk to the curator and see their Viking stuff.'

'Stuff?' Cathryn raised her eyebrows. But she was longing to see the ring that had been found in Farrshore — a link between the Vikings and the twenty-first century.

Magnus nudged Cathryn with his foot.

'If I drive as fast as you we should get there by Sunday morning.'

★   ★   ★

'Magnus and Peter and I are going to Inverness on Saturday,' she told Dolly later. 'Let me know if I can get anything for you.'

Rosie was doing a jigsaw at the kitchen table.

'Can I come?'

'No, you can't, and it's time you were away home,' Dolly said. 'Go and find your shoes.'

Rosie heaved a sigh but left the table.

Dolly sat down in her place.

'Magnus was telling me about this documentary of his.' She lowered her voice. 'I haven't told JD yet. He got mad about things that reporters wrote after his accident — facts they got wrong about the lifeboat service, and calling Farrshore 'a remote hamlet'.' She caught Cathryn's eye and laughed. 'Farrshore is the centre of the universe as far as JD's concerned and no-one is going to tell him otherwise.'

'This — guy I know, Daniel Barnard, he works in Lancaster but he thinks civilisation stops when you leave London.'

Dolly's eyes lit with interest.

'Is he your boyfriend? What does he do?'

Rosie came and leaned against Dolly.

'I know someone called Daniel.'

'Do you now?' Dolly gave her a quick kiss. 'See you in the morning, pet.'

When the door had closed behind Rosie, Cathryn said, 'Ex-boyfriend. We split up a couple of months ago.'

Dolly patted her hand.

'Well, my dear, what's for you won't go by you, as my mother used to say.'

Cathryn cast around for a change of subject.

'Is that your mother?' She pointed to a framed picture of a young woman in Edwardian dress.

Dolly got up and brought it over.

'No, it's me! 1975. Oscar Wilde — 'The Importance Of Being Earnest'. I'll show you my other photos some time, if you like. I used to be in rep. Then I met JD and he whisked me away to this remote hamlet.' She laughed, but her eyes were wistful.

'I'd love to see them. Do you miss it?'

'It was a long time ago. But if I could go back I'd do the same again. Marry JD, I mean.'

'Will he always be in a wheelchair?' Cathryn asked.

'We hope not. His injury just needs time to heal but he's not the most patient man in the world.'

'Are you talking about me?' Magnus stuck his head round the door.

'I could be. Magnus, you sit here. Dinner's ready.'

Dolly's Suggestion

After the meal, Cathryn sat watching a television soap while Magnus prowled around the sitting room in his stocking feet, picking up ornaments, putting them down, lifting up the lid of the piano and hitting a few notes, before coming to stand in front of the television.

'Do you mind? I'm trying to watch this,' Cathryn said.

'No, you're not. Your eyes are glazed over. How about coming out to see some real life? The real village of Farrshore.'

'That should take all of thirty seconds,' Cathryn scoffed.

'Dolly's great on the home comforts but I'm getting cabin fever. Let's go and frighten some seagulls.'

Cathryn ran upstairs to tie her hair back and to fetch her jacket and came back to find Magnus hopping on one leg, tying his bootlaces.

He seemed too big for the hall, like a teddy bear in a doll's-house. Cathryn smiled to herself at the image.

Magnus smiled back. He had a nice smile, she thought, straight white teeth and lines crinkling round his eyes.

As they passed Sara's house Cathryn remembered seeing Magnus standing in the doorway earlier in the week.

She opened her mouth to ask if he'd known Sara before, then she shut it again. It was none of her business.

'Which part of Canada did you say

you're from?' she asked instead.

'Vancouver Island. A piece of heaven on earth.'

'Why are you over here then?'

'Gotta go where the work is.'

As they reached the point where the steep path to the beach began, Magnus shouted, 'Last one down eats Peter's corned beef sandwiches tomorrow,' and then he was off, his boots throwing up showers of sand, his arms waving wildly to keep himself balanced.

The path was just big enough for two people side by side. Cathryn, brought up by the sea in Cornwall, was no stranger to racing over sand dunes and they arrived at the bottom at exactly the same time.

'I think we'll have to share those sandwiches,' she said when she got her breath back.

He put his hand on the back of her head. For a moment she thought he was going to draw her towards him and she took a step back.

'Your hair is coming out of that

49

horse's tail,' he said, letting his hand drop and looking over her shoulder. Cathryn turned to see Rosie sitting on her jacket, using it as a sledge to come down the path.

'Hey, are you going treasure hunting?'

'Does your mother know you're here?' Magnus asked. 'When's your bedtime?'

'I saw you coming out of Granny's so I followed you,' Rosie said. 'I don't have to go to bed for ages.'

'We'll look for treasure for ten minutes then we'll take you back. OK?' Magnus bent down and picked up Rosie's jacket and shook out the sand.

'There's a cave,' Rosie told them, struggling into the jacket. 'Not far. It looks like just the place to find something.' She grabbed a hand of each of them.

They spent ten minutes searching but found only shells and pretty stones. Rosie was disappointed until Cathryn told her that they were treasures from the sea.

★ ★ ★

'That wasn't much of a walk,' Dolly called from the kitchen as they opened her front door. 'You've only been gone twenty minutes.'

'Rosie saw us and followed us down,' Cathryn explained. 'We didn't want anyone to be worried about her.'

'It's hard to keep her away from the beach,' Dolly said. 'But we don't like her going down on her own. Come through. I was just going to put the kettle on.'

Sitting at the kitchen table, watching the sky darkening, Cathryn realised that they hadn't watched the sunset or chased any seagulls. She was about to say so when JD rolled his chair through from the back bedroom.

Dolly set the teapot on the table.

'I had an idea, Magnus. I thought of it right away after you got your

51

phonecall but I wanted to talk it over with JD first.' She hesitated. 'I was wondering if Tyler would like to spend the summer here.'

'That's an amazing suggestion, Dolly,' Magnus said. 'But . . .'

'In London you have to work and you can't let a wee boy out on his own. He could have the little room over the porch and he'd be company for Rosie. There are no children around her age in Farrshore.'

Magnus rubbed his hand over his face.

'That's extraordinarily kind of you both. It would be a huge weight off my mind. I'll try to spend more time here so you don't have to worry too much about him.' He stood up and kissed Dolly on the cheek before holding out his hand to JD.

That was lovely of Dolly, Cathryn thought, as she drank her tea. In one sense, of course, it would be a business arrangement, having Tyler as a paying guest, too, but she knew that Dolly's first impulse had been to help Magnus. But she couldn't help noticing that JD was being very quiet.

City Girl

Sara unfolded a duvet cover printed with a bright jungle scene.

'I thought Tyler would rather have this than the pink one with ballet dancers.' She laughed. 'Although Rosie's not keen on the ballet dancers, either. She'd rather have footballers, my mum would be horrified to hear!'

'How are your mum and dad? Still enjoying the sun?' Dolly asked.

'Dad certainly is. Not sure about Mum. Maybe the novelty of being in Spain all the time is beginning to wear off. She'd like Rosie and me to go out when school finishes.'

'And will you?'

Sara sat down on the bed.

'I don't see how we can.' She looked at her mother-in-law. 'I had a text from

Joe just before I came over. There's some sort of emergency and his next two weeks off have been postponed. I don't want to be away when he comes home.'

'That's a blow.' Dolly looked up from tucking the sheet in. 'Hope the emergency's nothing likely to be dangerous. I know it's a good job, but I've never liked thinking of him out there on the rig.'

'He won't be there for ever. Anyway, it would be better to go to Spain in October like we planned. Too much heat doesn't agree with Rosie.'

Sara and Joe longed to give their daughter a little sister or brother but it just hadn't happened and, at seven, Rosie was still an only child. Sara had been so down last year that, when the cottage opposite his parents came up for sale, Joe had suggested that they move. He would be with them just as often as he was in Aberdeen; Rosie would see more of her grandparents, and Sara would have Dolly's shoulder to lean on.

It made sense. Sara could still see that. The part-time job she'd taken when Rosie started school had always felt like a stop-gap, so it was no problem giving it up, and Rosie was thrilled to bits with her new home.

But Sara hadn't expected to miss living in the city as much as she did — just being able to shop, or go out for coffee, or have her hair cut without having to drive for miles. She couldn't say anything to Dolly; she was so pleased to have them near and, besides, she loved Farrshore and Sara wouldn't have hurt her feelings for the world.

'I'll give you a hand with the duvet.' Her mother-in-law's voice broke into her thoughts. 'I'll look out some of Joe's old games and books for Tyler,' Dolly went on. 'Oh, and we need a bedside lamp. Could you get one next time you're in Inverness?'

'Yes, of course.'

'You'll be going on Wednesday?' Dolly asked.

Sara carefully pressed the duvet's

fasteners together.

Her genealogy course was done only on the computer and, actually, she didn't have to go anywhere. But when she'd begun it a few months ago and decided to go to the library in Inverness for some background reading, Dolly had assumed that this needed to be a weekly occurrence, and Sara had let her think that so that she could spend a day away from Farrshore every week.

'Actually, I don't . . . ' she began but Dolly was cocking her head. 'That's JD. Needs something he can't reach, I expect. Thank you for your help, my dear.'

Sara followed Dolly downstairs.

JD had a clock in pieces on the kitchen table.

'I need my little tool kit. It was on the shelf there. Where is it? My house is being turned upside down and filled with strangers.'

Sara saw Dolly take a deep breath before reaching up to the back of the shelf.

'Here it is.' She put her hand on JD's

shoulder. 'You know we need to have . . . ' she began, but JD started rolling his chair towards the bedroom, taking several attempts before getting through the door and shutting it behind him.

'His mood changes like the wind,' Dolly said wearily. 'I know it's not easy for him . . . '

'It's not easy for you. You're looking tired. We'll have Tyler over to our house as often as we can,' Sara promised.

* * *

'Shall we bring some wine back to have with tonight's meal?' Magnus asked Dolly on Saturday.

Dolly clapped her hands.

'That would be lovely. Oh, why don't you ask your friend, Peter? And Sara and Rosie could come over. We'll have a party.'

Inverness was bigger than Cathryn had expected and the multi-storey car park was already busy.

'Are you going to the museum now, Magnus?' Peter asked.

Magnus might have made a bit more effort, Cathryn thought. It evidently hadn't occurred to him to brush his hair, which was sticking up in the now-familiar horns.

'Yes,' he replied. 'I thought maybe if I went up first, you could meet me about two and see the stuff.'

'Well, I've got 'stuff' of my own to do,' Cathryn said. 'Do you want to meet back here, Peter, for some lunch?'

Viking Gold

He was sitting on a low wall, waiting for her, when she'd finished her shopping.

'I found this nice little Italian restaurant down by the river,' he said.

Cathryn felt herself unwinding. Peter was funny and gossipy and by the time they were at the coffee stage she felt she'd known him for years.

'So,' he said, putting his elbows on

58

the table, 'do you have a boyfriend, partner, whatever? If you don't mind my asking?'

'I did have. Daniel. We went out for two years and I thought we'd get married one day, but, well, he told me last month he was seeing someone else.'

'What'd he want to do that for?'

Cathryn had to laugh at Peter's indignation.

'The thing is — ' She hesitated, her coffee cup halfway to her mouth.

'What?' Peter prompted.

'I heard that Daniel's new girlfriend was seen with someone else.'

'So do you think he'll come crawling back to you?'

It was an attractive picture.

'I doubt it. And I certainly wouldn't want him to,' she replied, wondering if that was the truth.

The waiter appeared.

'More coffee?'

Cathryn glanced at her watch.

'Thank you, but we have to go. May we have the bill?'

Peter took out his wallet as Cathryn reached for her purse.

'You can put that away,' Peter said.

'I'm going to pay my share,' Cathryn insisted.

'It's on Magnus,' Peter said. 'He gave us the money.'

Her eyes danced.

'I should have had something more expensive.'

Peter laughed.

'Magnus thinks a lot of you, anyway.'

'What do you mean?'

'He said you were a bit starchy in the flesh but he thought you were a natural on camera.'

'Starchy!' Cathryn expostulated.

'Can't think why he thought that. Anyway, he'll get a chance to change his mind. You'll be seeing a lot more of each other. He was telling me yesterday he's rearranging his summer so that he can spend more time in Farrshore with his son.'

★ ★ ★

Magnus was waiting in the foyer of the museum.

'Good lunch?'

'Very, thank you. Vintage champagne, steak. No, only kidding.' Peter handed over the change.

Magnus stuffed the money in his pocket.

'If the dig goes well we'll patronise the fanciest restaurant in town,' he promised. 'Dancing girls, you name it. But first, work. Come and see the . . . the Viking artefacts.' He led the way downstairs.

Cathryn suppressed a smile. Magnus had obviously made a big effort not to say 'stuff'. But, when she held the ring, 'Viking artefact' didn't seem the right way to describe it either. This was something that someone had actually worn eight hundred years ago.

'What do you think, Miss Fenton?' the curator asked. 'Viking gold, certainly. For a man or a woman?'

Cathryn laid the ring in the palm of her left hand and traced it gently with her right forefinger. It was made of five fine strands of gold, plaited and twisted into a circle.

'It's so delicate.' Hard to reconcile with strong men adventuring across unknown oceans. 'May I?'

She slipped it on to the ring finger of her left hand, moved it to the middle one. It still slid around easily.

'Too big for me.' She took it off and passed it to Magnus. He kept hold of her hand for a moment.

'You've got slim fingers,' he said, 'so that doesn't prove anything. A Viking wench's may well have been thicker.'

'But we know the men wore rings, too,' Cathryn pointed out.

If only the ring could speak, what stories it could tell, she thought.

Dolly's Party

In Dolly's sitting room a dining-table that had been folded against the wall now dominated the room.

Magnus introduced Peter and handed Dolly the wine he had chosen.

'I'll just have a wash,' Cathryn called to Dolly, 'and then I'll give you a hand.'

'No hurry, my dear.' Dolly came into the hall. 'Sara and Rosie have been helping.'

Cathryn freshened up quickly, made up her face and gathered her hair into a loose knot. She changed into a cotton skirt patterned in various shades of green and clipped on a pair of vintage green and gold earrings.

Rosie had put a name card and some wild flowers in an egg-cup by each place.

Cathryn found herself next to Sara.

'Dolly was telling me you're doing a course in genealogy,' she said. 'Are you enjoying it?'

'It was just something to do when we came here,' Sara replied, 'but when Magnus found out about it he asked me to trace his ancestors. He says they came from around here. When it's for real, not just theory, it's fascinating.'

Cathryn digested this information along with Dolly's casserole.

'And you do that online? From birth certificates and so on?'

'Mostly.' Sara glanced at Dolly, her face slightly pink, then turned back to Cathryn. 'But I've drawn a blank with finding Magnus's relatives. I'm not sure what to do next.'

JD seemed to be in good form, with Rosie on his right-hand side, her voice suddenly loud and clear.

'It's funny, Grandpa,' she was saying. 'There's a boy at my school called Daniel, and Cathryn's boyfriend is a different Daniel. Daniel Barnard.'

Liability

Everyone looked at Cathryn, who wished she could hide under the table. She could say that Rosie's information was out of date, but it wasn't anybody's business.

'Rosie, come and help me cut up

64

your mum's cheesecake,' Dolly said. She smiled at Cathryn apologetically. 'Little pitchers have big ears.'

Peter dived to her rescue by asking JD if Farrshore had changed since he was a boy and JD was happy to talk at length on the subject. He talked about the Lodge and how his good friend, the previous owner, had had to sell up.

'Some actor's bought it, Sara tells me,' he said. 'From one of those soap things. It will just be a passing fancy, mark my words.'

At ten o'clock Peter got up to go. Magnus stood up, too.

'I've got an early start for London tomorrow but shall we walk Peter home, Cathryn?'

'I've never walked at night without streetlights,' Cathryn said.

'It's not dark yet,' Dolly said. 'But I'll give you a torch, that road's bumpy.'

Peter was staying with an old man and his sister who evidently went to bed early. Their house was in darkness and Peter was glad of the torchlight as he put the key they'd given him in the lock and said goodnight.

They were hardly out of the yard when Cathryn, despite the pale crescent moon and the torch, stumbled over a stone and would have fallen if Magnus hadn't caught her.

'Woman, you're a liability,' he said.

He tucked her arm through his.

'If you fall, I fall, too.'

Cathryn kept her eyes on the bobbing circle of torchlight.

* * *

The next morning Cathryn reached for her laptop and Googled the website of MM Films. There was an impressive list of their productions and a picture of Magnus apparently taken at an awards ceremony, wearing a suit and a tie, with his hair slicked down.

When she went downstairs, the front door was open and Magnus's suitcase was on the step. By his car, Magnus was apparently being plagued by Rosie to let her sit in the driving seat. Cathryn stepped outside to watch as he opened the door with a flourish then leaned in and turned the key so that the little girl could work the indicators and flash the lights. He acknowledged Cathryn with a half wave.

'You OK? Good. See you in a few days. Keep digging.'

A peep on the car horn made him bend down again.

'Must get down the road, Rosie,' he said, and she got out and came over to Cathryn while Magnus folded himself into the front seat and drove off.

'Look!' Rosie clutched at her hand. 'Magnus's case. It's still here.'

They ran out on to the road waving and shouting, but Magnus tooted the horn in farewell and kept on driving.

Unexpected Encounter

'That's it, Liz. Did I ever tell you that you're brilliant?' Magnus put his diary down and smiled at his PA.

'It wasn't hard. There's a couple of times you can't avoid having to be away but the rest of the time you can be with Tyler.'

'I'm looking forward to it. I hope he is. Right, I'm going to stretch my legs and get something to eat. Can I get you anything?'

Liz shook her elegant grey head.

'I'll have something later. I've got a few loose ends to tie up.'

I'll have to go and buy some clothes, Magnus thought gloomily, thinking of the suitcase left on Dolly's doorstep. Distracted first by Rosie and then by the sight of Cathryn standing smiling in the doorway, he hadn't given it a second thought. But the shops he looked into were crowded and he couldn't face them, so he bought a sandwich and headed towards the nearest park.

The warm weather had brought the crowds here, too, and there was an oppressive smell of hamburgers and fried onions, so he turned and went back to the office block, wishing he were five hundred miles further north.

As he passed the reception desk he overheard a man saying, 'Daniel Barnard. I have an appointment.'

Magnus slowed down.

The receptionist smiled.

'Yes, Mr Barnard. Fourth floor. The lift is over there.'

Magnus had been going to walk up the stairs but decided he would take the lift, too. Daniel Barnard wasn't an unusual name but it wasn't a common one, either — could this sharp-suited city boy really be Cathryn's boyfriend?

Surprised

'After you.' Magnus followed him in. 'Who are you here to see? We're getting out on the same floor. I can point you in the right direction.'

'Oh. Thanks. I'm seeing Andrea Thomas. She's — '

'I know her.' Magnus nodded. 'The producer.' He paused, leaving a question in the air.

'She's looking for a presenter for a new history programme.' Daniel was clearly excited. 'Someone mentioned my name and she asked me to come in for a chat.'

They were nearly at the fourth floor.

'Excuse me asking — do you know Cathryn Fenton?'

Daniel looked surprised.

'Yes, we — yes, I do. Where is she?'

Where is she? That was an odd question for a boyfriend to ask.

'We're working on something together,' Magnus said as the lift doors slid open.

'What? Where?' Daniel spoke quickly.

'It's an ongoing project.' Magnus evaded the second question again, wishing he hadn't struck up the conversation. If Cathryn didn't want Daniel to know where she was he wasn't going to tell him. Besides which, he wasn't going to talk about the dig.

'This is my office. Andrea's there on

the right. Good luck.'

He saw Daniel taking in the name on his door.

'MM Films. Well, give Cathryn my best, won't you?'

Magnus went in, feeling Daniel's eyes boring into his back.

3

Rough Diamond

Cathryn stood up and stretched her back. After looking down at the ground for the last hour she appreciated seeing the blue sky, and the hills above her just beginning to turn purple.

She walked over to the edge of the field and looked down on Farrshore, finding it hard to believe that not very long ago she'd never heard of it.

The cottages had originally been part of a big estate, JD had told her, which over the years were sold off.

From her bird's-eye view, Cathryn could make out a tiny Dolly cleaning the front windows of her cottage, and Sara hanging out washing in her back garden.

It was interesting that Sara was researching Magnus's ancestors. A different kind of archaeology, in a way.

Cathryn resolved to get to know Sara better, because she wasn't much older than Cathryn herself and it would be good to make a new friend. However well Sara got on with Dolly and JD she was bound to feel rather isolated, with Joe away, and no-one of her own age nearby.

Beyond the cottages Cathryn could see the road that dipped down to Farrshore Lodge. She smiled as she remembered JD's description of the new owner: *an actor from one of those soap things.* But which one? Cathryn couldn't remember.

Back in the dig she asked Peter if he knew.

''Hardcastle'. Not that I watch it myself, you understand, but it's my mum's favourite. An everyday story of skulduggery and back-stabbing, as far I can make out. Garvie Hammond plays the head of a huge family, a pretty tough guy.'

'That sounds a million miles from

Farrshore. Hope he's not like that in real life.'

'Rough diamond with a heart of gold. That's what he's like in 'Hardcastle'.'

'You know an awful lot about it for someone who doesn't watch it!' Cathryn teased.

'An interesting description. But probably accurate.' Thelma startled them by joining the conversation.

Cathryn wouldn't have had Thelma down as a soap fan and said so.

'I'm not. I don't even have a television.' Thelma didn't stop what she was doing, carefully sifting earth through a large sieve. 'But I had to spend a ridiculous amount of time in the dentist's waiting room recently and the only magazine that wasn't about golf was one of those with gossip articles. I read about Garvie Hammond in it, and there was a picture of his recent wedding.'

'And?' Peter prompted, giving up any pretence of working himself.

Thelma put down her sieve and

stood up, as if addressing a classroom.

'He left school at fifteen and was apprenticed to a builder. A casting agent spotted him sitting on his motorbike at traffic lights and offered him an audition. He's been acting ever since. He was in Hollywood briefly but prefers to work here. He was married before when he was very young. No children.

'He's well known for the amount of charity work he does. It's a second marriage for Gina Hammond, too — she's taking his name. They both wanted a home in the country and intend to spend as much time as possible up here. Garvie has been written out of 'Hardcastle' for three months. Gina wants a break, too. She's been acting professionally since she was nine.'

Cathryn and Peter stared at Thelma, their mouths open.

She laughed and bent to her work again.

'It's a blessing and a curse, having a

photographic memory,' she said. 'I have no desire to remember all that nonsense, but there it is. I could tell you who made her dress and what colour her shoes were but, frankly, I find that kind of thing extremely boring. Now, this is better.' She picked out a shard of pottery and stared at it. 'Not what we're looking for, but intriguing nevertheless.'

'Well, I'll be after an autograph for my mum,' Peter said. 'This summer's turning out to be even more interesting than I thought it would be.'

Thelma shook her sieve again.

'I don't expect our paths will cross, however much time they spend here.'

Cathryn wasn't so sure. She couldn't see Dolly not giving her new neighbours a welcome, whatever JD's opinion of them might be.

*   *   *

'What do you think Tyler will be like?' Rosie asked for the umpteenth time since she had heard he was coming.

'He's Magnus's son so I'm sure he'll be nice,' Dolly said. 'Though I expect things here will seem strange to him at first.'

'Will he want to play with me?'

'I'm sure he will, darling,' Dolly replied, hoping she was right. 'Now, how do you want to ice those cupcakes? Pink or chocolate?'

'Both,' Rosie decided. She dragged a stool over to the cupboard and stood on it to reach inside.

'We've got white sprinkles and chocolate stars.'

'That sounds good, Rosie Posie.' JD rolled his chair through from the back bedroom and negotiated the kitchen door.

Rosie crouched on the stool and then manoeuvred herself on to JD's lap.

'Take me over to the table, Grandpa,' she commanded. 'Having a wheelchair in the family is very handy.' She slid off his knee. 'Thank you for the lift. Does Tyler like cupcakes?' she asked, turning to Dolly.

'We'll make some more to welcome

him.' Dolly glanced at JD, remembering his comment that she was filling the house with strangers. He wasn't looking well. He had tossed and turned most of last night and his face was grey.

Rosie chattered on about teaching Tyler to play football and showing him her favourite place on the beach.

Don't let him have an outburst in front of Rosie. Dolly realised her fingers were clenched tight around her wooden spoon.

'Farrshore's a busy place these days.' She forced herself to speak brightly. 'Magnus, Cathryn and everyone up at the dig. Tyler. And the new folk coming to the Lodge.' Too late she remembered that was a touchy subject with JD, as well. He was missing his lifelong neighbour, the old laird, whose increasing frailty had forced him to sell up and move south.

But the fight had gone out of JD today.

'All change.' He shook his head. 'All change.'

Dolly put on the final swirl of icing.

'You finish these off, Rosie, then we'll leave Grandpa to have a wee sleep. Let's take some cakes over to your mum.'

Rosie put some cakes aside and then carefully chose another, covered it generously with sprinkles and stars and put it on a plate.

'This special one is for you, Grandpa.'

JD pulled her pigtail gently and smiled.

'I'll look forward to it.' He leaned back in the chair and closed his eyes.

'I can hardly remember Grandpa walking,' Rosie said as they crossed the road. 'When will he walk again?'

'It could be a long time yet. Backs are very tricky,' Dolly said, waving to Sara at her window.

She came to meet them at the door.

'Daddy's coming home next week!' she said excitedly to Rosie. 'I've just had a text.'

'Well, that's good news.' Dolly handed over the tin of cupcakes. 'JD will be pleased.'

'I'll put the kettle on,' Sara said. 'Isn't it sunny? Let's sit in the back garden.'

A Touching Picture

On days like this, when the seagulls swooped in a cloudless sky and the smell of the sea arrived on the faintest of breezes, Sara could appreciate the charms of Farrshore.

She watched Rosie reach through the garden fence to pick a stalk of bog cotton and wave it in front of the kitten, Bee, who had followed them over.

It was a good place to bring up a child, she had to admit. Rosie looked so healthy — she had grown so fast in the last few months that the T-shirt and skirt she was wearing were quite skimpy. She must have a look through Rosie's clothes and decide what she'd grown out of.

They could have a day out together in Inverness and do some shopping; get

Rosie kitted out before Joe came home. When he was here he wouldn't want to go very far away. He liked to spend time with his father, trying to keep JD's carpentry business ticking over and taking him out, pushing the wheelchair up and down the hilly roads with his strong arms.

What on earth could she tell Joe when he asked about her life in Farrshore? Of course it was lovely, at this moment, to sit in the garden she was trying to make, Rosie playing happily and chatting with Dolly about this and that. But it felt like someone had pressed the 'pause' button on her life.

The days passed in a blur — not because she was busy, but because she wasn't. And it would be even worse in the winter. Short days, long dark evenings. Bad weather preventing any journey that wasn't necessary. Any escape.

Goodness. She was feeling sorry for herself. Sara picked the paper case off a cupcake and pulled herself together to respond to Dolly.

'I hope you'll get to know Cathryn better,' her mother-in-law was saying. 'You must be about the same age. Did you know she was brought up by the sea in Cornwall? But she's quite the high-flying career girl now — gets asked to speak at conferences all around the world. Farrshore must seem very quiet to her, dull, even. Not that she's said anything, but I wonder.'

A piece of cake seemed to get lodged in Sara's throat. She swallowed hard.

'And Tyler,' Dolly went on. 'I was just saying to Rosie that he'll find it strange here at first. A different way of life.' She chuckled. 'I did myself, many moons ago.'

And what about me, Sara had to press her lips together to prevent herself from shouting. I may not be a high-flyer or a little boy far from home but did you ever think I'd find it strange and quiet and dull? A pang shot through her. It seemed disloyal to Joe to think like that, but she couldn't help how she felt.

At least when they were in Aberdeen there had been some structure to her day. She left the house with Rosie in the mornings for her part-time job in administration for an oil company. She would never get used to living in Farrshore and trying to work from home. It wasn't really work, anyway. Just fiddling about on the computer trying, without success, to trace Magnus's family tree.

Dolly was still talking about Tyler.

'Magnus says he's a lad who loves being outdoors, so I think he'll be all right. And a summer of running around outside will be so good for Rosie. Really, it's providential. A friend for Rosie during the holidays.'

Rosie has friends, Sara thought. It's just that none of them live within three miles of Farrshore!

Hearing her name, Rosie came over and sat on the ground in between their chairs.

'Bee doesn't want to play any more,' she said. 'She buzzed off. I think she might have seen a fieldmouse.'

She leaned her head against her mother's knee and reached out to hold Dolly's hand.

It would make a touching picture to anyone seeing them, Sara thought. But she hardened her heart.

She had a couple of weeks to plan how she would put it to Joe. But she was going to tell him, calmly but firmly, that she wanted to move back to Aberdeen.

*　*　*

Magnus looked up at the arrivals board. He'd been so anxious not to be late that he was nearly an hour early. He wandered into one of the shopping concessions that sold magazines and sweets. There was a bright array of comics but most of them seemed to be for girls. Maybe Tyler would like a computer magazine instead. Or one on fishing — he went out with his grandfather on the lake near their home. But probably he'd rather actually fish than read about it.

Magnus picked up several chocolate bars before remembering that in the last picture he had of Tyler he was sporting braces on his teeth. Maybe chocolate wasn't a good idea.

He left the shop without buying anything.

The truth was he didn't know what Tyler would like. He only saw his son about every three months and it was hard to keep up to speed with him. For several years his favourite thing was playing with Lego but now the box lay abandoned under his bed. Lucky that Magnus had thought to ask what he wanted before buying him more for his tenth birthday.

Not that he had actually been there for Tyler's tenth birthday. Nor his ninth. He tried to remember if he'd managed his eighth. They'd had a wonderful time last Christmas, though, tobogganing and skiing and eating Magnus's mom's home-made dough-nuts.

But his last visit hadn't gone so well. Arriving unannounced as a surprise, he found that Tyler was just leaving for a camping weekend with a schoolfriend.

He went to check the board again. The plane had just arrived. He positioned himself at the gate so that he would see Tyler the minute he turned the corner.

Coming Home

'That's Scottish air, Tyler. We've just crossed the Border into the land of our ancestors.' Magnus turned to look at his son, suddenly thrilled at the thought of the links going from this ten-year-old boy back through the generations.

'But this isn't where your great-whatever came from, is it?'

'No, no. We've nearly three hundred miles before we get there. Your great-great-grandfather. His name was Finlay Macaskill. He . . . '

'Finlay. Is that who I'm called after for my middle name?' Tyler interrupted.

'That's right.' Finlay would have been his son's first name if Magnus had had his way. 'He was from Sutherland, right at the top of Scotland. His father had a croft — that's a little farm. But Finlay didn't want the crofter's life and ran away to sea. That's the story that was passed down, anyway.'

'So how come we're Canadian?'

'Finlay ended up as a deckhand on a trawler off British Columbia. Presumably he came ashore and liked the look of the place. Met your great-great-grandma. We'll never know how it happened.'

'And you're making a film about it?' Magnus laughed.

'Wouldn't that be something? No, I'm making a documentary about the Vikings.'

'They're the guys with horns on their helmets, eh?'

'I'll have to get Cathryn — she's one

of the archaeologists I'm working with — to put you right on that one. No, they didn't have horns, but I think you'll like hearing about them.'

'But can we find out more about old Finlay?' Tyler asked. 'I like the sound of him and his fishing boat.'

Family Tree

Magnus turned to look at his son. He had Magnus's blue eyes and shape of head. It looked as if he was going to be tall, too. His hair was dark, like his mother's, and his wide smile reminded Magnus of the woman who had walked out on them both when Tyler was just a few months old. But the pain of that had gone now, as far as Magnus was concerned. How could he regret his brief marriage when it had given him Tyler?

'I've got someone looking for his birth certificate,' he said. 'We'll try to make a family tree.'

'Cool.' Tyler put on his iPod and

leaned back, his fingers drumming on the knee of his jeans.

Magnus wondered if Tyler ever thought about the mother he couldn't remember. He seemed very happy with his grandparents, but it was only natural that one day he would ask Magnus more about her. Tyler's family tree would include his mother. There was no getting away from that.

They'd had two good days seeing the sights in London before heading north and staying a night in Berwick-upon-Tweed. Now they were on the last lap.

Magnus thought of stopping off to visit Edinburgh, but it was a long way to Farrshore and he wanted Tyler to see the countryside in daylight. He'd like to explore Scotland's historic capital city some time, though. Perhaps Cathryn would come down with them. It would be new to her, as well.

He tapped his son's hand and Tyler removed an ear-phone.

'We'll stop somewhere for lunch soon.'

'What's Scottish food like?' Tyler

asked. 'Grandad said I'd be eating something called haggis.'

'I haven't tried it,' Magnus said. 'But Dolly — that's who we're staying with — is a good cook.'

'And who's this Rosie you were talking about last night?'

'Dolly's granddaughter. She's about seven. She's looking forward to you coming.'

'My friend has a kid sister,' Tyler said. 'She's always trying to get him to play with her dolls.'

Magnus saw a sign for a craft shop and restaurant and slowed down.

'I think Rosie's more interested in football.'

Tyler put the iPod in his backpack.

'I bet she doesn't know how to play basketball.'

Ships That Pass

They were about twenty miles from Farrshore when Magnus became aware of a large car a few hundred yards ahead. He caught up with it but there was no room to overtake on the narrow road. Further on, an oncoming van forced both cars to squeeze into a passing place.

Tyler whistled.

'That's some car. Looks like the Queen might be in it.'

'I hadn't heard she was coming to Farrshore for her holidays,' Magnus said, 'although I'm sure Dolly would give her a good welcome and put the kettle on.'

He was surprised how much he was looking forward to being back with Dolly and JD. And Cathryn. He was on the move so much usually that it almost felt like coming home. Especially now that Tyler was with him.

* * *

Cathryn could see that the e-mail was from Daniel and was headed *Where are you?* Below it were two other messages from him.

91

They were in the inbox from her work e-mail that she only looked at now every couple of weeks.

Her students and colleagues knew that she would be away for six months, although they didn't know where. The Professor wanted to keep the dig under wraps so she had told only close friends and family where she was going.

Cath — you seem to have disappeared off the face of the earth — have you gone time-travelling? Saw Lucy but she wouldn't tell me where you are, and bumped into your friend Magnus Macaskill — he told me you were working together but he wouldn't tell me where either. What's all the mystery? Please get in touch. We really need to talk. Daniel.

Daniel had met Magnus! When had that happened? Magnus hadn't said anything, although she hadn't seen him much since he came back from London. He spent most of his time with Tyler, hill-walking or beach-combing.

Cathryn read the e-mail again.

During their two-year relationship, marriage had never actually been mentioned but she had assumed that they were heading in that direction. But the last time she saw Daniel he had told her that he thought they were getting too serious and he wasn't ready to settle down. Had he changed his mind?

She could hear Magnus, Tyler and Rosie in the kitchen below, in heated argument over a board game.

The screen blurred before her eyes. She had pushed Daniel to the back of her mind. Being busy at the dig, and living with strangers who were becoming friends, was a kind of oasis away from her normal life. Even after hearing from Lucy that Daniel's new relationship might be over she had been able to keep her thoughts at bay. But now it seemed that 'normal life' was catching up with her.

She stood up quickly, knocking over the rather flimsy bedside table holding her laptop, which fell against the bedroom door. She picked it up. The screen was blank.

Magnus called from the foot of the stairs, 'Are you all right?'

Cathryn opened her door.

'I dropped my laptop. I think it's broken.'

'Bring it down. Let's have a look at it.'

'See,' Cathryn said, putting the computer and its lead on the kitchen table. 'I can't get it to go on again.'

Magnus reached for it but Tyler was there before him.

'I'm pretty good with Grandad's. He's always pressing the wrong keys and I have to sort it out.' He looked around the kitchen. All the sockets seemed already to be taken. 'Can I take it to my room and plug it in?'

'Of course, please do,' Cathryn said gratefully. 'I don't want to lose all the work I've got on it.'

Tyler left the room with the computer, and with Rosie at his heels.

Cathryn sat down and picked up a counter from the board game.

'Sorry to interrupt your game. Who was winning?'

'Not me. The kids ganged up on me. I'm practically bankrupt.' Magnus put on a pathetic face.

Cathryn laughed.

'I came down at just the right time, then.' She turned the counter over and over in her hand.

'Magnus.' She stopped, trying to think what to say next. 'I had an e-mail from my friend, Daniel. He said he'd met you.'

'Ah, yes. Your Mr Ear-ring.'

'Where on earth did you meet him? And how did you know he knew me?'

'He was at reception in the block I have my office in. I heard him say his name and remembered Rosie mentioning it that night we all had dinner here. We went up in the lift together.'

'But what was he doing there?'

'I gather he had an interview with a TV producer.' Magnus shuffled through his toy money.

'But why? He's a history lecturer.'

'Cathryn.' Magnus put the money down. 'You might not want to be on television but everyone else in the country does. Or so it seems. And history programmes are very popular. I expect Mr Ear-ring is hoping to be a presenter.'

'Daniel. His name is Daniel. Did you tell him about your documentary?' Through the window behind Magnus Cathryn could see the beginnings of another beautiful sunset.

'And have the Professor come after me with a rusty sword? What do you think? No. If Daniel finds out you're in Farrshore he didn't find out from me.

'So is he an ex-boyfriend? Was Miss Big Ears Rosie misinformed?'

'Yes. Probably. I don't know.' As the sun began to dip towards the horizon the last shafts of evening gold coming through the glass made her blink.

Magnus stood up and walked over to the window.

'We never did finish that walk in the sunset that Dolly recommended.' He turned back to look at her. 'Shall we try again some time?'

'It does look beautiful.' Cathryn looked down at the counter, avoiding saying yes or no.

She and Magnus were just two ships passing through Farrshore's night. Before the end of the year she would be back in Lancaster and Magnus would be off on his travels again.

Magnus was looking at her, a smile in his dark blue eyes. He seemed to be waiting for an answer.

He was attractive; she couldn't deny that. With his broad shoulders silhouetted against the window and his red-blond hair illuminated in the evening light, that likeness to a story-book Viking struck her afresh.

But he was just being friendly, wasn't he? One passing ship signalling to another.

Cathryn looked away first.

'Some time, maybe,' she said. 'I wonder if Tyler's having any luck with my laptop.'

'He's a whiz at all those things,' Magnus said with fatherly pride. 'All these new gadgets. I can't keep up with them.'

Tyler and Rosie could be heard clattering noisily down the stairs.

'Tyler's mended your computer.' It was Rosie who was proud of the boy's achievements now.

'That's brilliant, Tyler. Thank you very much.' As Cathryn took it from him something occurred to her.

When had Daniel sent the other e-mails? She wondered if they had all been sent after he met Magnus.

If so, it was possible he only wanted to talk to her because he thought she had media contacts that would help his own future plans.

A Surprising Proposal

Joe laid out the last strip of paper on the table and slapped paste on the back of it.

'OK. Let's get this one up.' They manoeuvred it into position and stood back to admire their handiwork. The room looked lovely with the pale yellow and white striped wallpaper and freshened-up paintwork.

A week of Joe's leave had gone by already.

He'd arrived with pots of paint and rolls of wallpaper — and lots of enthusiasm for decorating first Rosie's bedroom and then their own. So Sara's plan to wait until his second evening, cook him his favourite meal and tell him she didn't want to stay here got overtaken by the whirl of activity.

One of the things she loved about Joe was the way he went at everything full tilt — whether it was sweeping her off her feet when they met at a mutual friend's party nine years ago, or renovating the old boat currently parked at the side of the house, or painting Rosie's bedroom in the colours of her favourite football team. How could she tell him that she wanted to leave the home they'd just spent time improving?

'I think Rosie's pleased with her room, isn't she?' Joe said. 'Not that she's been in it much except to sleep.'

'Tyler's being very patient with her. She's following him around like a wee dog.' Sara smiled as she caught sight of Rosie laying down two jumpers as markers in the garden and adopting a goalkeeping position. Tyler was twirling a football round on the tip of his finger.

'She likes having a surrogate big brother.' Joe followed Sara's gaze and went over to knock on the window and wave at the pair of them.

He turned back to Sara and put his arm around her.

'And maybe one day she'll have a little brother or sister.'

'I'm resigned to that never happening.' Sara twisted round so that she could look at him. 'It's the best way. I try not to think about it.'

'You've got other things to think about, haven't you?' Joe dropped a kiss on her forehead. 'Rosie. The garden. You're making a great job of that — it was a wilderness before. And your course. That gets you away to the big city once a week.'

Sara took a deep breath. Now was her chance.

'No, Joe. I don't have to go down to Inverness for my course. I go just to be among people, among buildings. I get a bit stir crazy up here. Rosie's at school most of the time and I can't keep going over to Dolly's. I'm just not very good at being on my own.'

Now that she'd told him, said it out loud, her small deception didn't seem the big deal it had been in her head. It actually sounded perfectly reasonable.

'Oh, Sara, I'd no idea you felt like that.' Joe took his arm away so that he could see her face. 'There may be a way round it.'

'Move back to Aberdeen?'

'What? No. Is that what you want? It's not as bad as that, is it?' Joe looked stricken.

'Well, sometimes I feel that's what I would like,' Sara admitted. 'What was your idea?'

Joe sat down on the edge of the bed.

'I don't know how you'll take this now,' he said. He rubbed his face with his hands, then looked up at her.

'It's Dad. He's suggested that I come home and take over from him.'

'Leave the rigs and work in JD's business?'

'Yup. Obviously Dad's not been able to do anything for weeks now and he doesn't want to lose all his contacts.'

'Could we afford to do that?'

'It would mean some belt-tightening. But I've done almost twenty years on the rigs. I never intended to do it for ever. Dad's forced my hand. What do you think?'

Sara sank down beside him. It was too much to take in all at once.

There was a bang on the window.

'Daddy, come and play football with us. Pleeease. You can go in goal.'

Joe got up.

'Let's sleep on it, Sara. Let's think what would be best — for all of us.'

He went out of the door leaving Sara staring after him.

4

A Surprise Announcement

JD put down his spoon. 'No one makes soup like your granny,' he told Rosie. 'Is there any left in the pot?'

Dolly had tried a new recipe — carrot and ginger — and it looked as though it was a success. It seemed to have put JD in a good mood, anyway.

Rosie and Tyler were tucking into second helpings of bread and cheese.

'What are you two up to this afternoon?' Dolly asked.

'Going up to the dig, I s'pose.' Rosie didn't share Tyler's newfound passion for the Vikings and their possible settlement, but if that's where he wanted to be, then she'd be right there, too.

'What do they actually do up there?' JD asked her.

'Dig, of course,' Rosie said, 'with wee spades. And they have sieve things they shake the earth through. Tyler thinks it's cool to watch.'

JD laughed.

'Cool, is it? How about I come with you?'

'You want to go up to the site?' Dolly tried not to sound surprised. To date JD had shown little interest in what was happening above the village. 'But, dear, I'm not sure I can push the chair up the hill.'

'We've got Rosie and this lad here to help,' JD said, laying his hand on Tyler's arm. 'He's been showing me stuff about the Vikings on that computer of his. I'd like to see this dig for myself.'

The wheelchair was self-propelling but there was no way JD could attempt the steep and stony path. Even with Dolly behind one handle and the children at the other they made slow progress. JD had always been a big man and the weeks of inactivity had left him heavier.

Dolly looked down at him. His hair was iron-grey but still as thick as when he was a young man. She tucked the label of his jumper in and patted his shoulder.

'We're doing fine, but let's have a rest at the corner.'

She put the brake on and knelt down so that she was at JD's eye view as he looked out to sea.

As part of the lifeboat crew sent out to a yacht in difficulties, he had been thrown against the side of the boat when his harness snapped. Dolly would never forget the phone call that told her he was being air-lifted to hospital. She shuddered at the memory. Perhaps JD knew what she was thinking, because he squeezed her hand.

But there was the sea, blue-green and calm, as though nothing bad ever happened on it. And here was JD, in a wheelchair, but alive, and looking the brightest she'd seen in weeks. She squeezed back.

'My dad says that my great-great-grandad ran away to sea,' Tyler piped up.

JD looked at him with interest.

'Relative of mine did the same. Great-uncle John. Sometimes the sea just calls out to you and you can't resist. I never wanted to go on the fishing boats, but I was a lifeboat man.'

'That sounds exciting.'

'Yes, I had my fair share of excitements, you could say.'

Rosie hopped up and down.

'Tell him about the dog, Grandpa, the big dog you rescued.'

As JD related one of Rosie's favourite stories, Dolly's thoughts drifted to Joe and Sara. How wonderful it would be if Joe decided to come home for good. She'd thought that Sara would be even more thrilled than she was herself at the idea but, strangely, Sara hadn't wanted to talk about it.

There was nothing wrong with their marriage, Dolly was sure. It might be difficult to adjust from seeing your husband two weeks out of four to him being home all the time, but Dolly didn't think that was Sara's problem. Maybe she was worried about how they would cope financially. She and JD had their own money worries so they couldn't help. Thank goodness for the dig and her lodgers.

She looked at Tyler, listening intently to JD's tale. Rosie had taken to the boy like the proverbial duck to water and tried to be as much like him as possible, imitating his drawl and begging an old baseball cap from Joe because Tyler wore one. He was very patient with Rosie. He seemed quite happy to stay endlessly in goal while she practised scoring, although he had been heard to mutter that basketball was a much better game.

Now he was talking to JD about his father's work.

'The film Dad's making here is just part of a documentary about the Vikings. They go all over the place, you know. He says I can go with him to

Orkney when he's there next month.'

Dolly froze.

JD's dislike of the media, following their intrusion into his life after the accident, meant that she had tried to keep the fact of the film from him. She'd asked Magnus and Cathryn to keep it quiet, but she knew she couldn't conceal it from JD for ever.

Now he astounded her.

'I was asking your dad about it last night,' he said. 'When you were over at Joe's,' he added, glancing at Dolly. 'He's asked me if I'd like to be in that film of his. Tell folks about the history of Farrshore. I'm the only one who knows the old yarns, now the laird's gone.'

Dolly found her voice.

'And what did you say?'

'Said I'd have to talk it over with you, Dolly, love. What do you think?'

'I think it's wonderful.' Dolly got to her feet. 'Now let's go up there and see what's happening.'

* * *

109

The children were at the dig a few days later when Cathryn found the comb.

'What's so good about it?' Rosie whispered to Tyler. 'It's all muddy and there's a bit broken off.'

'I don't know, but everyone seems very excited,' Tyler whispered back.

'It's a Viking comb, made of bone,' Cathryn said, overhearing them.

'I wouldn't like to use it.' Rosie twirled her pony-tail round her finger.

'Nobody will be using it,' Thelma said, before Cathryn could reply. 'Can you stand back please, Rosie. Professor, I have to say I don't think children have any place at a dig.'

'But they're interested,' Cathryn protested. 'They're not doing any harm.'

Professor Gillanders smiled at the children in his usual friendly way.

'Why don't you go and tell Magnus about the comb?' he suggested. 'It's finishing time here, anyway.'

As they packed their tools away in the caravan Thelma said, 'I mean it, Gil.

110

They're nice children but they could contaminate the scene. I must insist that if they come up here they sit quietly at the edge of the field. There are plenty of opportunities for them to speak to Cathryn or any of us if they want information.'

'Very well, Thelma. I'll have a word with Magnus and with Rosie's parents.' The professor looked as if this wasn't a task he relished.

'I'll do it if you like, Professor,' Cathryn said. 'I'm sure they'll understand.'

Neither Magnus nor the children were at Dolly's when Cathryn got back. She had a shower and was in her dressing-gown with a towel round her head when there was a tap at her bedroom door.

Dinner in Achbuie

Magnus was leaning against the jamb. 'Like your hat.' 'Very funny. I'll just dry my hair and get dressed. I'll be down in a minute.'

'Talking of hair, is it true about the comb?'

'Yes, it is.' Cathryn relaxed against the door, her eyes shining. 'Oh, Magnus, it more than likely means that they did settle here. It all made sense theoretically. The high position on the cliff, the coins that were found. But this is real evidence.'

'Perhaps we could talk about it over dinner.'

'Yes, I'll be down in a minute.' Cathryn made to shut the door.

'I mean, I thought we might go out to dinner, just the two of us. I believe there's quite a good restaurant in Achbuie.'

'But won't Dolly have been cooking?'

'I took the liberty of mentioning my invitation to Dolly earlier. Is it a date, then?' He raised his eyebrows at Cathryn. She noticed for the first time that his hair had been smoothed down and, although he was still in jeans, he was wearing a freshly ironed white shirt.

'Well, you seem to have sorted it between you,' Cathryn said, grinning.

Magnus turned to go downstairs, then he looked back.

'And what was all that about the kids not going near the dig?'

Cathryn took a step towards him.

'I hope they weren't upset?'

'Tyler was, a little. Rosie's delighted but trying not to show it.'

The towel was threatening to slip off Cathryn's head. Magnus reached out and straightened it, his finger brushing against her cheek.

'Dad.' Tyler was at the bottom of the stairs looking up at them. 'I'm going to Rosie's for tea. OK?'

'Fine with me. See you downstairs then, Cathryn.'

*   *   *

'What's going on here?' Cathryn asked an hour later as they approached

Achbuie and saw crowds of people walking under colourful bunting stretched across the small main street.

'I told them you were coming, Cath. Aren't you impressed?' Magnus glanced at Cathryn, grinning.

'It's a festival.' Cathryn peered up as a banner came into view. '*Achbuie Summer Festival. Art exhibition, live music, hill-running competition* . . . And there's a sign saying *Festival Parking*.'

'Well spotted,' Magnus said, turning down to the right.

The field that had been requisitioned for the occasion was almost full, and the restaurant, when they found it, was completely full. There were no free tables until nine o'clock.

'I'm sorry, Cathryn.' Magnus looked sheepish. 'I never thought of booking.' He looked at his watch. 'Two hours. We can't wait that long.'

Cathyrn saw a queue of people.

'I think that's a fish and chip shop.'

'Fish and chips! I was going to wine and dine you.'

'I thought we were just going to talk about the comb?' Cathryn could smell the hot vinegar as people passed with their paper parcels.

'Well, yes. But in more fancy surroundings than a chip shop.'

'Come on.' Cathryn tugged at Magnus's arm. 'We can take them to the beach, look, down there. There are some wooden tables and benches.'

'Well, it's either that or begging Dolly for a sandwich.' Magnus allowed himself to be propelled along the pavement.

Cathryn stopped short outside a shop apparently selling everything from newspapers to tents.

'Would Tyler like one of those?' She pointed to a red, white and blue board with a net attached. 'He could use it to practise his basketball.'

'Great idea.' Magnus got out his wallet.

'No, I want to get it,' Cathryn said. 'As a thank you for sorting out my computer. And to make up for Thelma's outburst today.'

'Thelma was probably right. Don't worry about it. This would certainly distract Tyler from the dig.'

Cathryn stood on the pavement with the basketball board while Magnus went into the chip shop.

Fish and chips tasted best outside, she thought as they started to eat. Magnus, despite his earlier comments, seemed to be enjoying his alfresco dinner, too. He looked around at the beach and the little harbour.

'I like the décor. This was a good idea.'

Cathryn was going to ask Magnus if he would be getting a cameraman back to the site, and she tried to summon up enthusiasm to talk about the comb. But this was the first time that she and Magnus had ever been really alone and she found herself thinking about him instead.

'What? Have I got ketchup on my nose?' Magnus asked, and Cathryn realised she must have been staring.

'No.' She picked up a chip and put it

down again. 'How is Sara getting on with finding your ancestors?'

'I'm beginning to think that the story of old Finlay coming from a croft in Sutherland and running away to sea is just Chinese whispers. Sara can't find any trace of him. Tyler's disappointed. He'd love to think he had some connection to this place.'

'He's settled down so quickly.'

'He's an adaptable kid. He's had to be.' It was Magnus's turn to stop eating. He traced a pattern on the table with his finger. 'His mom decided she wasn't cut out for motherhood when he was just a few months old. He's lived with my parents ever since.'

'I'm sorry.'

'It's a long time ago now.'

'Does she — your — Tyler's mother, does she see him?'

'No. She does want to know about him and I send her photographs, but that's it. She lives in some kind of commune in California — she always was what you might call a wild child.'

'I'm sorry,' Cathryn said again.

Magnus looked up and smiled.

'No need, really. It was like the end of the world at the time and I thought I'd never trust any woman ever again, but you have to move forward, especially when you have a child to bring up.'

Cathryn wondered if there was a particular woman who'd restored his faith, but that wasn't really a question she could ask. She wiped her fingers on a paper napkin.

'Are you ready for dessert, madam?' Magnus stood up. 'They sell ice-cream in that funny little store. What do you say we get one and take a walk along the beach?'

'Sounds good.' Cathryn pulled herself together. 'And I'll tell you about my Viking comb.'

New Neighbours

JD bounced with frustration in his wheelchair.

'No, laddie. That's not the way to do it.'

He looked up at Joe, perched on the old fishing boat at the side of the house.

'That hull is more damaged than it looks. I told you to sort that out first.'

'I am sorting it out,' Joe replied mildly.

'It looks to me like you're just fiddling about up there.'

'I've worked out what I need to do with the rudder so I thought I'd do that today.' Joe's tone was less mild this time.

'But the hull — '

'The hull can wait, Dad.'

Round at the front of the house, Dolly listened with one ear to Sara and with the other to her husband's raised voice. They'd all just had Sunday lunch and now Dolly and her daughter-in-law were doing some weeding. Dolly knew that more than anything JD wanted to be up on the boat with Joe. Before his accident they had been a good team.

Now she sympathised with both of them.

'Ask Grandpa if he would like another cup of coffee,' she said to Rosie, hoping to distract JD.

Rosie came back, pushing the wheel-chair.

'No, he does not want coffee,' she said. 'And he says he'll leave Daddy to get on with his tomfool repairs.'

JD was too het up to be embarrassed by this report.

'Park me here in the shade, Rosie. And leave me in peace, all of you.'

'Mum,' Rosie whispered to Sara, 'Grandpa said to Daddy that maybe asking him to come home for good was a bad idea. What did he mean?'

Sara looked exasperated.

'I wasn't going to tell you yet. Daddy might leave the rigs and come and work in Grandpa's business.'

'And be here in Farrshore all the time?'

'Sssh. Yes. Maybe.'

'Oh, Granny, wouldn't that be great?'

'Yes, it would, it would be lovely.' Dolly didn't dare say anything else, given the look on Sara's face. Joe was due to go back to the rig in a couple of days. She hoped that a decision would be made before he went. 'Rosie, look, there's Tyler for you.'

Really, all she seemed to do these days was change the subject, try to prevent arguments, and pour oil on troubled waters.

Tyler was looking to the left as he came through the gate.

'There's two people coming along the road. One of them looks like that detective guy, Sherlock Holmes.'

Rosie rushed to see for herself.

'So he does.' She giggled, although she had no idea who Tyler was talking about. 'He's got a funny hat on.'

Tyler began to laugh as well.

'Don't be rude, Rosie,' Sara said. 'Go and play round the back, both of you, if you can't behave.'

'Do you want to come and practise shooting?' Tyler asked and Rosie skipped after him over to Dolly's house, where the basketball net had been fixed to the wall.

As the strangers came closer Dolly could see that the woman was slender with classically beautiful features and dark hair in a chignon. She wore a green and white summer skirt and a short green linen jacket. She stopped and smiled.

'Hello. I'm Gina Hammond. My husband and I have just moved into Farrshore Lodge.'

The man touched his deerstalker cap.

'Garvie Hammond. Good to meet some neighbours.' He pushed open the gate.

Dolly stood up and hastily dusted her hand on her skirt.

'Dolly MacLeod. I live across the road there. This is my daughter-in-law, Sara. Welcome to Farrshore.' For a moment Dolly felt as if she might giggle herself as she took in Garvie's plus-fours and that hat, at odds both with Gina's city elegance and with his own marked London accent.

'How are you settling in?' Sara asked and, as Gina started to tell her that they were camping in two or three rooms for the moment while they sorted themselves out, Garvie looked around and spotted the wheelchair parked beside the porch.

'Hello, there!' He moved forward, his hand held out. 'Garvie Hammond, Farrshore Lodge.'

JD had been dozing. He opened his eyes to see, not Sherlock Holmes, but a man ridiculously attired in gamekeeper's tweeds, an interloper thinking he could take the old laird's place in the community.

He kept his hand by his side.

'Well, Mr Hammond, if you are as good a man as the previous occupant of the Lodge you'll do well. It's not just an acting job, you know.'

Garvie Hammond laughed, not at all abashed.

'I'm not here to act.'

'So why the fancy dress?'

'JD!' Dolly was horrified to overhear this conversation.

'Mr Hammond, do come into the house and have coffee or a cold drink.'

'Garvie. Call me Garvie, Dolly. Lovely name, Dolly.'

They went inside, leaving JD glowering after them.

* * *

Dolly picked out six large brown eggs and put them in a box. Gina Hammond had found out that Dolly kept hens and had asked if she could buy eggs on a weekly basis. But this box, plus a large bunch of flowers from the garden, was to be a housewarming present and an apology for JD's rudeness.

There hadn't been an opportunity to apologise or explain yesterday. Sara's kitchen seemed to have been filled with Garvie's presence, holding court, talking about his plans for the Lodge. Then Joe appeared and Garvie found out about the boat and insisted on going out to look at it.

Gina asked questions about life in Farrshore and about the history of the Lodge and seemed genuinely interested in the answers.

JD fell asleep in his chair and didn't wake up until the Hammonds had gone.

Now, after lunch, leaving JD with one of his old lifeboat cronies for company, Dolly made her way down the hill to the Lodge.

The laird had never married and he never entertained. So although JD sat in his kitchen many a night exchanging stories, Dolly had only been in the Lodge once, when the laird's house-keeper had showed her over the whole building.

Her memory was of dark wallpaper and furnishings unchanged for many decades.

She found Gina sitting at the huge kitchen table, an array of paint samples and brochures in front of her.

'Of course, the sensible thing would

have been to do all the renovating and decorating and then move in,' she told Dolly, 'but once the house was ours Garvie couldn't wait. There's so much to do. The plumbing is practically Victorian and the wiring's not much better. But in other ways it's been well looked after. The roof is sound, Garvie says. He's climbed out on to it to check.'

'You're not doing all the work yourselves, surely?' Dolly asked.

'No, no. The electricians have started already. I'm trying to decide on colour schemes. But there are so many rooms. I've done up several houses in my time but I think this one might be a challenge too far. I know Garvie would like the whole tartan Balmoral look but I'm not so keen.'

'You must do it your way, darlin'.' Garvie came through the door and dropped a kiss on Gina's head.

Gina smiled at him.

'I was just going to make tea. Look at the lovely flowers Dolly brought us.' She got up to put the kettle on.

A Job For Sara?

Garvie sat down in her place.

'So how's Dolly this afternoon?'

'I'm fine. But I wanted to apologise to you, Mr Hammond, Garvie, for JD's behaviour yesterday. It was less than welcoming. He hasn't been himself since he had an accident and he is sore about the Lodge being sold, but that's no excuse.'

'No offence taken. I've heard worse.' Garvie's blue eyes danced. 'I hope I can improve on first impressions. I want to get on with my neighbours and I liked the look of JD very much. Maybe it would help if I left my new suit in the wardrobe next time I see him?'

Dolly laughed, relieved.

Gina moved some of the sample books so that she could put the teapot down.

'Actually, the paint and wallpaper stage is a long way off. Did you know that we bought the Lodge with all its furniture? The first thing I have to do is decide what to keep. There are some lovely pieces but equally some I could never live with, and others that are falling to bits. Garvie can move furniture around so we can see where it looks best, but I really need someone to walk round the Lodge with me to help clarify things in my mind, and keep a note of what we decide.'

Dolly had a flash of inspiration.

'If you didn't have anyone else in mind, how about Sara, whom you met yesterday? She's very efficient and practical and I sometimes think that she finds time hangs a bit heavily here.'

Gina clapped her hands together.

'Oh, would you ask her, Dolly? If she likes the idea tell her to come down so that we can sort out hours and so on.'

Dolly almost ran back up the hill and after the briefest of knocks she burst through Sara's door.

'Coo-eee. It's me.'

Sara and Joe both came through to the hall.

'Is everything all right, Mum?' Joe asked.

Dolly nodded vigorously.

'Sara, how would you like to work for the Hammonds? The Lodge was left in a bit of a state and Gina could do with an extra pair of hands. She says if you're interested to — '

Her voice trailed away.

Sara was looking far from pleased.

'You want me to go and clean for Gina Hammond?'

'It's not like that,' Dolly said. 'She's lovely and she needs some help to — '

'No,' Sara said. 'No. I could do with some work but I've got enough cleaning to do in my own house, thank you very much.'

'Why don't you go and see her anyway?' Joe put his hand on Sara's arm. 'As Mum says, she seems to be very nice. And you know you've often wondered what the Lodge was like inside.'

Sara shrugged him off.

'I am not going to be a skivvy. For anyone.'

She grabbed her jacket from the hallstand.

'I'm going out. Don't come after me, Joe.'

She slammed the door behind her.

In The Lodge

Cathryn and Thelma left the site together that afternoon.

'I must go and type up my notes about the comb. I've just scribbled something so far.'

'Your computer's none the worse for its fall, then?' Thelma asked.

'I've got my own IT consultant.' Cathryn laughed. 'It's all sorted out. Now Tyler's actually got JD interested in the internet. He's gone from declaring it 'a waste of time' to saying 'Dolly, come and look at this' every five minutes. It's really very funny.'

They stopped to admire the view out to sea.

'Not missing Daniel any more?'

Thelma looked sideways at her friend. She and Cathryn went back a long way — to before Daniel's appearance on the scene.

'I don't have time to think about him.'

'And of course you had your dinner date with Magnus,' Thelma said slyly.

Cathryn laughed.

'If you can call fish and chips dinner.'

'I asked the professor if he knew anything about Tyler's mother. He said he understood that she'd left Magnus 'to find herself' when Tyler was just a baby.'

Cathryn didn't say that she had heard this from Magnus himself.

'But Tyler's, what, ten?' Thelma went on. 'Magnus should have put that behind him now.'

'It can't have been easy.' Cathryn didn't like the idea of the professor and Thelma gossiping about Magnus and maybe about herself. She changed the subject.

'Is that the children down on the beach?'

'Where?'

'I thought I saw a flash of red.' She wasn't sure now if she'd imagined it or not. 'Rosie was wearing red shorts this morning.'

As they passed the village hall, a notice on the window caught Cathryn's attention and she stopped to read it. Volunteers were needed to tidy and decorate the hall before the forthcoming ceilidh. Those interested in helping were asked to see Dolly MacLeod.

'I'd be happy to join the hall work party,' she said to Dolly as she took off her outdoor shoes in the porch.

'Thank you, dear.' Dolly didn't sound quite like herself.

'Is everything all right?'

'I've just put my big foot in it.' She gave Cathryn a brief account of the misunderstanding between Sara and herself. 'And then she just walked out. I daren't go over and see if she's come back.'

'I can think of an excuse to pay a visit later if you like. But it looks like it's going to rain. She won't stay out if it's wet.'

* * *

Sara marched down the hill, not caring where she was going.

How dare Dolly barge in like that and think that she would be delighted to be offered a cleaning job! Well, that settled it. She wasn't going to stay in Farrshore a minute longer than necessary. JD could find someone else to go into business with him. Joe would stay on the rigs. And she would see if her old firm would have her back.

She shut her mind to what Rosie's reaction would be.

'Sara?'

Sara was so deep in thought that she didn't see Gina Hammond at the bottom of the Lodge drive. She had a pair of secateurs in one hand and there was a basket at her feet.

'Hello, there! I'm cutting roses and

some of this greenery. Your mother-in-law brought us such a beautiful bunch of flowers from her garden earlier I thought a few filled vases would cheer the Lodge up.'

Sara's mind was in a whirl. She had liked Gina Hammond yesterday and she didn't want to be rude to her. She was bound to ask what Sara thought of the proposition and she tried to think of a way of politely turning the job down.

'Did Dolly have time to ask you if you'd consider working for us for a few weeks?' Gina put down the secateurs and came out into the road.

'She said you were looking for someone to clean but — '

'Clean? No, no. When all the dirty work is finished — the electrics and the heating and so on — we'll get in a firm of contract cleaners. What I want is someone to — look, why don't you come in and see for yourself?'

Sara followed her down the drive. She couldn't help feeling rather thrilled that at last she was seeing inside the big white house.

From the basement to the attic Gina didn't spare Sara an inch. There was even a small ballroom, its walls adorned with antlers.

All the while she talked gently about how she needed someone to make lists and keep track of what furniture she wanted to keep and if it needed any repairs, what to sell, give away, make a bonfire of . . .

Sara was fascinated by everything, especially the ornate wardrobes and the china cabinets. By the end of the tour she felt her fingers itching to start making those lists.

'Well, you're exactly the person we need.' Gina laughed when Sara told her. 'When can you start?'

Sara would have hurried back up the hill as fast as Dolly had earlier if it wasn't for her flip-flops. It started to rain and she had difficulty in keeping them on her feet. She took her jacket off and held it over her head.

The rain increased so she kept her head down and concentrated on putting one foot in front of the other. As she went down her own path she cannoned into Joe.

'Joe, I'm sorry,' she burst out. 'I've seen Gina Hammond and — '

'I can't find Rosie and Tyler,' Joe interrupted. 'I've just phoned Mum and they're not with her. Look at that sky. I think we're in for a storm.'

5

Tartan Carpets

'The weather here changes so quickly.'
Gina Hammond stood watching the
rain as it bounced on the paving
outside. 'There wasn't a cloud in the
sky when I was picking the roses earlier.
I hope Sara didn't get too wet going
home.'

'She wouldn't want to be outside in
that.' Garvie joined Gina at the window.
A flash of lightning briefly illuminated
the wall of the neglected kitchen
garden. Seconds later came a loud
rumble. 'Listen to that thunder.' Garvie
made to pull the blind down.

'Don't.' Gina put her hand on his
arm. 'I rather like looking at the wild
elements of nature when we're warm
and dry in here.'

'Yes, at least the old boy made sure

the wild elements stayed outside. Wouldn't want to have a leaky roof in this part of the world.' Garvie turned back to the box he had just opened. 'It will be good to have all this sorted out.'

'With Sara's help that shouldn't take as long as I thought,' Gina said as she lifted out dinner plates wrapped in newspaper. 'Don't go mad opening boxes, darling. Just kitchen stuff. I don't want our belongings to get mixed up with what was here already.'

'So Sara liked the idea?' Garvie abandoned the unpacking and went to sit at the kitchen table.

'Yes. She said she couldn't wait to start, to have something to do. Isn't that great? She didn't exactly say so, but I gathered that she's missing city life.'

'Well, I'm certainly not. I wouldn't care if I never saw a city street again.'

'You know you can't hide up here for ever. Think what fun you'll have telling the others on 'Hardcastle' about your Highland lodge.'

Garvie got on so well with the cast of

the soap opera he'd been starring in for years that Gina knew, when his three months' grace was up, he'd be looking forward to going down to London to start filming again.

'We'll invite a few of them up to stay when we get organised. Or all of them — the house is big enough,' he added lavishly. He looked at Gina, his eyes mischievous. 'Of course, they'll be expecting tartan carpets and cases of stuffed trout. I hope you don't disappoint them.'

'I'm afraid I will. I don't want the place to look like a hotel. But don't worry. It can look Scottish without going over the top. What do you think of the antlers on the ballroom wall?'

'You're not going to get rid of those?'

'They did make me shudder a bit the first time I saw them. But Sara's reaction was the same as yours. I think I'd be rather unpopular if I consigned them to the bonfire.'

'Good for Sara. I should think so. They're part of the history of the house.'

Gina held up her hands, smiling.

'The antlers stay. And you can have your study as tartan as you like.'

Garvie had earmarked a room off the back hall as his own. The walls were hung with old black and white framed photographs of the estate in its heyday, and the lingering smell of pipe smoke attested to the fact that the previous owner had spent much of his time in there.

'I can wear my new suit in that room with no-one to tell me off.' He laughed but there was a wistful look in his eyes.

Gina remembered their visits to Edinburgh's most expensive tweed shop and Garvie's excitement when the suit was ready.

She leaned back on her heels and reached up to kiss him.

'I think you look lovely in it,' she said gently. 'I'll take a picture of you wearing it for the study wall.'

'Wait until we get this little beauty and she can be in it, too.' From the table Garvie lifted a photograph of a golden retriever pup. 'Do you want to come with me tomorrow? They phoned to say she was ready to pick up.'

'Ooh, yes. The kennels are farther up round the coast, aren't they?'

'About twenty miles apparently.' He cupped his hand around Gina's face. 'I think you look lovely, too. We are going to be happy here, aren't we, sweetheart?'

'I'd be happy anywhere with you,' Gina replied. 'But I love it here. Yes, we're going to be very happy — you, me, and Achbuie Highland Toffee the Third.'

'I'm looking forward to taking her out,' Garvie said. 'Let's hope it's not so wet tomorrow.'

Missing!

Sara stared at Joe, rain dripping from her hair and eyelashes. She tried to think back to earlier in the afternoon. When had she last seen Rosie and Tyler?

'I thought they were practising basketball over at Dolly's.'

'They were. When Mum stopped hearing them she assumed they'd come back here.' Joe felt Sara's arm. 'You're soaking. Do you want to get changed? I'll go across to Mum and Dad's — meet me there and then we can organise a search party.'

A search party! Sara tried to gather her thoughts as she took off her wet clothes and threw the disintegrating flip-flops into the bin. She hadn't seen Rosie and Tyler as she left the house earlier, but then she'd been so upset by the thought that Dolly expected her to skivvy for the Hammonds that she hadn't seen anything. Sara would have some apologising to do to Dolly later on.

First, though, they had to find the children.

As the thought of her little girl out in the storm came to Sara's mind, she shivered. Surely Rosie and Tyler would have the sense to shelter somewhere. But where?

'Rosie! Tyler!' she called as she crossed the road. Her words were snatched away in the wind.

'Sara.' Dolly's eyes were full of tears as she put her arms around her daughter-in-law. 'I should have checked that they were back in your house.'

'It's not your fault, Dolly. They'll be OK.' Sara turned to Joe. 'What should we do? And where's Magnus?'

'At the site, as far as I know. You and Mum go up — maybe they're with him. I'll go the other way. Let's meet back here in half an hour if we can't find them. Dad . . . '

'I'll hold the fort.' Dolly knew the effort it took JD to say that in a calm voice, knowing that he wasn't able to take charge and lead the search as he would have done a few months ago. 'Somebody has to be here if they come back by themselves.'

Sara appreciated his positive words. She had begun to think of all the things that might have happened to

Rosie and Tyler. Who said the countryside was safer than the city? You could be lost on the hills for days, break your legs tripping over rabbit holes, fall off the edge of the cliff . . .

She bit her lip, trying not to cry.

* * *

Cathryn heard voices in the hall and then the front door banging.

In the sitting room JD was rolling his wheelchair backwards and forwards.

'Is something wrong?' Cathryn asked. Pent-up energy was coming off JD in waves.

'We don't know where Rosie and Tyler are. Joe thought they were here. We thought they'd gone across the road. No-one's seen them for at least a couple of hours.'

Cathryn put her hand to her head, trying to think.

'Thelma and I left the site just before the rain came on. We stopped at the corner of the path. I thought I saw a flash of red down on the beach. Do you think it could have been Rosie?'

'Dolly and Sara have gone up to that site of yours to find Magnus. Joe's gone down the hill — could you go and find him, lass, and tell him what you've told me?'

Cathryn grabbed the nearest jacket, a large blue one, from the hooks beside the door.

'I know where Rosie's favourite cave is,' she said. 'I bet she's there.'

'Joe will go with you,' JD called, but Cathryn had gone.

A wet cliff path was a different proposition entirely from the sandy one Cathryn and Magnus had raced down a day or two before. This time, Cathryn had to crouch, reaching for the tall grasses on either side to keep herself from falling as she slithered to the bottom.

The visibility, too, was different. In the Highland summer evening light they'd been able to see all the way along the shore, where the foamy edges of the sea lapped on to the sand. Now, the sky was dark with storm clouds and, although she couldn't see them, Cathryn could hear the threatening roar of the waves as they crashed on the wet beach.

She stopped, wiping her face and pushing her wet hair off her forehead, trying to get her bearings.

There was an opening in the cliff face.

'Rosie! Tyler!' She peered into the gloom.

Nothing.

She felt her way along the cliff face. Another opening. She called again.

'Cathryn?' The name came out on a sob as Rosie's sandals clapped over the cave floor towards her. 'Tyler and me are so cold.'

Cathryn edged into the dark cave and saw a forlorn little figure standing in the shadows. She peered into the blackness.

'Where is Tyler?'

'Here.' Tyler could hardly speak through his chattering teeth. He wore a short-sleeved T-shirt, and as Rosie looked the better clad of the two Cathryn took off the jacket she was wearing and held it out to him.

'Here.' She helped him push his arms through and zipped it up. 'I think it's your father's. I just took the first one that came to hand.'

That made Tyler smile a little.

'Tyler gave me his hoodie to wear,' Rosie said, and Cathryn involuntarily reached out and squeezed the little boy's shoulder. Tyler ducked his head, pleased, then lifted up his arms in their huge sleeves and waggled them at Rosie.

Cathryn held out her hands to them.

'Let's try to get back. Everyone's worried about you.'

Tyler began to sound anxious.

'We went to look for Viking treasure. I thought we should run home when it started to rain, but Rosie was frightened of being out in the thunder.'

'It's good you were together.' She sought to distract them. 'Did I ever tell you that the Vikings had nicknames? Yours could be Tyler Wet-Hair. Or Tyler Big-Jacket. And Rosie would be Rosie Red-Head.'

Tyler managed another smile.

'What about Dad?'

'Ah, well. There was once a real Viking called Magnus, you know, and his nickname was Magnus Bare-Leg.'

Tyler laughed this time.

'Why was he called that?'

'No-one's quite sure. Possibly because —'

'I could be Rosie Bare-Leg,' Rosie interrupted, hopping with one leg in the air.

'So you could.'

There was a sudden slithering and scuffling from outside the cave and then Magnus burst through the entrance, his hair wild and on end.

'Cathryn, you found them. Oh, well done!' He grabbed both children in a bear-hug and pulled Cathryn towards him with his free arm. She could feel his warmth through her thin blouse, which was soaked.

'Thank you, Cath.' He held all of them close.

She let herself be held for a moment longer and then pulled away, reaching for Rosie's hand again and setting off up the path.

Dolly and Sara were hovering anxiously at the top.

'Hot baths all round,' Dolly said as Sara bore Rosie home, and Joe appeared and was relieved to be told there was no harm done before following his wife and daughter.

Tyler tugged at Cathryn's arm.

'You never finished telling me about you-know-who.' He slid his eyes sideways towards his father.

Cathryn laughed.

'Come on. You have that hot bath and I'll tell you later.'

'What? Tell you what?' Magnus demanded.

'It's a secret,' Tyler told his father. 'Between me and Cath.'

'I must go and check the hall,' Dolly said a few days later. 'See that the rain didn't get in during the storm.'

'Shall I come with you?' Cathryn offered. 'I promised to be one of the cleaning-up party for the ceilidh, remember.'

'Of course, my dear,' Dolly replied. 'I'll be glad of the company.'

The women chatted amicably as they made their way up to the hall.

'How are things with you and Sara?' Cathryn wanted to know.

'Oh, they're grand,' Dolly said thankfully. 'She started at the Lodge this morning. Rosie's over with us. She's a bit subdued, what with her dad going away and all the shenanigans on the beach the other day, so she's quite happy just to sit and play Ludo with JD.'

As they reached the hall, Dolly took a key from her pocket and opened the door, and their chatter died on their lips as they surveyed the scene before them.

The canvas chairs piled up in the middle of the floor were wet through and the whole floor was awash with gritty rubble.

'The storm must have dislodged some of the tiles,' Dolly said. Her shoulders drooped dispiritedly. 'We'll never be able to sort this out in time. We'll just have to cancel the ceilidh.'

'Sort what out?' Magnus appeared in the doorway. He stopped and gave a low whistle. 'I see what you mean.'

Dolly turned to him.

'I'm sorry, Magnus. JD was telling me you were planning to do some filming at the ceilidh.'

'For some local colour.' Magnus nodded. 'I'll think of something else. Look, Dolly, what can we do to help? We could put those chairs in rows to dry them out.'

'Let's do that now, and come back later with some of the neighbours,' Dolly said. 'Many hands make light work. Then I'll have to put up a notice saying the ceilidh's off, and tell the band not to come — oh, dear, all sorts of things.'

Cathryn and Magnus exchanged sympathetic looks and started to pull apart the piles of chairs.

The hall was really the village school, Dolly told them on the way home, bought by local people when it closed three years ago, but after the fund-raising efforts to buy it there wasn't much money left over to turn it into the kind of building the community needed.

'For one thing we want somewhere here in Farrshore that can be part of the Achbuie summer festival. That's been such a success,' Dolly was saying, when they were hailed by Garvie and an excitable puppy.

Disaster

'Meet Achbuie Highland Toffee the Third,' Garvie said proudly.

'My, that's a grand name,' Dolly said admiringly.

'This is Toffee's first proper walk,' Garvie went on, 'so I don't want to let her off the lead.'

'Come away in and have a cup of tea. Cathryn, Magnus?' Dolly invited, hoping that her lodgers' presence, along with the dog's, would help smooth any awkwardness at this second meeting between JD and Garvie.

It seemed to work. Toffee, after an initial jumping around, settled on the tartan rug that trailed on the floor from the arm of the wheelchair and went to sleep, with an entranced Rosie beside her. The talk was amicable, about dog breeds and training, while JD leaned down to stroke the top of Toffee's head.

'How was the hall?' he asked Dolly, remembering where she'd been. 'Dolly was worried there might have been storm damage,' he added for Garvie's benefit.

'Oh, disaster!' Dolly told them what had happened. 'So the ceilidh will have to be cancelled. We'll talk about it later,' she said, suddenly aware that Garvie didn't seem to be listening but had put down his cup, crossed the room and picked up one of the photographs from a small side table.

'This you?' He looked over at Dolly. She nodded.

'Trod the boards, did you? I didn't know that.'

'No reason why you should. I just did rep. Never hit the big screen, or the small one, come to that,' Dolly said with a laugh.

'But live theatre is much more difficult than television. You just get one chance. What play was it?'

Dolly got up and went over to him.

''The Cheviot, The Stag And The Black Black Oil'.' She picked up another frame.

'And this was 'The Importance Of — ''

'Excuse me.' Rosie had followed her grandmother. 'Could I take Toffee for a walk, please?'

Garvie hesitated. Dolly could see that he didn't want to let his baby out of his sight.

'I don't think so, Rosie,' she said.

'It's Complicated'

Magnus stood up. 'Cathryn and I will go, too. Just up to the site and back.'

Garvie sat down again at the table and poured himself another cup of tea. He seemed genuinely interested in Dolly's reminiscences, and for once had nothing to say about himself.

'I must tell Gina we have a repertory actress for a neighbour.' He waved away Dolly's denials. 'It's like riding a bike, Dolly, riding a bike.'

'Never done any of that yourself, then?' JD asked, basking in Dolly's reflected glory.

'Don't think I'd have the courage, JD. Television's a doddle in comparison.' Garvie stood up. 'I think I'll go and meet Toffee. Your granddaughter's welcome to come to the Lodge any time she likes to see her.'

He turned round, one hand on the door.

'A ceilidh's a kind of dance, isn't it? How about holding it at the Lodge?'

Dolly stared at him.

'At the Lodge?'

'First time I've had a ballroom of my own,' Garvie said. 'Seems a shame to waste it. Come down tomorrow and we'll have a chat about it.' He closed the door behind him.

''A ballroom of my own',' JD mimicked, but his tone was mild. 'He seems to know a good dog when he sees one, though.'

★   ★   ★

Sara switched on her computer. As she waited for the machine to warm up, her mind turned again to Joe's parting words.

'We must make a decision next time I'm back. Without fail.'

There had been no time for a proper discussion before he left, no time to tell him all about the Lodge and Gina Hammond. All their attention had been focused on Rosie.

Behind her JD was now teaching his granddaughter to play draughts.

She clicked on to a site that let her look at birth, marriage and death records.

As part of the work for her genealogy course she was researching a branch of her own family tree. Goodness, look at that. She must remember to tell her mother that one of her ancestors had had eleven children. Sara sighed, reading down the list of names. All those babies . . .

That research was much more straighforward than Magnus's request to find his great-grandfather. Magnus had told her the name. Finlay Macaskill; the date of birth, 1883; and the possible place of birth, Sutherland. These details should have been enough to start with, but she had drawn a blank.

'What are you doing?' JD rolled up behind her.

Sara indicated the screen.

'I have to put a family tree together. Look, Rosie, one of Granny Anne's great-aunts had eleven children!'

JD moved closer.

'So you can look at birth certificates and all that kind of thing on the computer?' Since Tyler had shown him how to access the internet he had been fascinated by what you could see without moving from your own home.

Sara nodded.

'I'll show you. Do you know your father's name and date of birth?'

JD told her, and watched how she called up the birth certificate. He read it with interest.

'Can I have a go?' he asked. 'If it's not interrupting you.'

'Of course. Why don't you make a note of all the names and dates and I can start to draw up a tree for you?' She moved to let him be in front of the computer and went to take JD's place at the draughts board.

'Does Tyler have a mum?' Rosie asked, picking up a counter.

'I think it's a bit complicated,' Sara said. 'His dad isn't married to his mum any more.'

'But why doesn't he live with his mum when his dad's away? He lives with his grandpa and grandma.'

'He's happy with them, isn't he?'

'Ye-es. But it must be funny not seeing your mummy. I wouldn't like it.'

Sara leaned across the table and squeezed Rosie's hand.

'It's just the way it is for them. I expect Tyler's used to it.'

Rosie considered.

'Maybe Cathryn could be his new mum.'

'I think Cathryn's too busy being an archaeologist to be anyone's mum. Where did you get that idea from?'

Rosie looked sheepish.

'Tyler and me just wondered.'

'Anyway, Cathryn's got a boyfriend, hasn't she? Daniel something?'

But Rosie's attention was on the board now. She laid her draught down.

'Your move, Mum.'

'Sara.' JD turned round. 'I've looked up a great-uncle of mine. Rosie, it's the one I was telling you and Tyler about, the one who ran away to sea and was never heard of again. John Finlay MacLeod. I can't find any marriage or death certificates for him.'

'Maybe he's not dead,' Rosie said.

JD laughed.

'We're a long-living family, Rosie, but I don't think so. He'd be, let's see, a hundred and twenty-eight if he was still alive. He was born in 1883.'

Sara went over to the computer and peered at the screen.

'That's the year Magnus's great-grandfather was born. Maybe they knew each other, went to school together. How frustrating. If only he was still alive, Rosie, we could ask him.'

Toasting Marshmallows

'Mum said we can have a picnic in the garden.' Rosie looked up at Tyler. 'We can help ourselves to whatever we like.'

Tyler sighed and then nodded.

'Cool,' he replied.

Rosie was a good kid, really. She'd never asked him to play dolls with her and she was happy to practise basketball for as long as he did himself.

But he felt restless this afternoon. The weather had turned very hot, reminding him of home and summer camp, where his friends would be now, hiking, kayaking, building dens. And here he was, having to stay within the confines of a back garden with a little girl.

They picked out a packet of chocolate chip cookies, a punnet of strawberries, a big bag of pink and white marshmallows and two cans of fizzy drink, and took them out to the garden.

The flattest piece of ground was over

by the back fence where also, conveniently, were the large stones for Sara's intended rockery. Two they could use as seats, and another one became a table for the feast.

Rosie showed Tyler the deliciousness of a sandwich made by squashing a strawberry and a marshmallow between two biscuits. Tyler drank his pop in one go, and when Rosie had finished hers they placed one can on a fence post and tried to hit it off with the other.

After ten minutes Tyler cast around for something else to do.

'Say, Rosie, you ever toasted marshmallows?'

'Yum.' Rosie licked her lips. 'Do you put them in the toaster?'

''Course not. You make a fire and hold them over the flame on the end of a fork or something.'

'I'm not allowed to touch the matches.'

'We don't need matches.' Tyler looked around for some little sticks. 'I know how to start a fire without one. We did it at summer camp last year.'

∗ ∗ ∗

Down at the Lodge, Sara and Gina stood in the drawing room. Its chintz curtains and striped wallpaper would once have been pretty but now they were marked and faded. The mirror above the mantelpiece had dulled and the furniture was coated with dust. But Gina could see beyond all that.

'I love the fireplace. Can you imagine this room all done up with a real log fire? And look at the plasterwork on the ceiling. It will take some cleaning but it will be beautiful, I know it will.'

Sara admired her enthusiasm, and her tenacity. Of course, the Hammonds had the money to make the Lodge's transformation a reality, but it would also take vision and a lot of hard work to see it through.

'There's another cabinet full of china in here,' she said. 'The laird's family look like they were great hoarders, but I suppose when you've so much space you can just hang on to everything.'

'Some of it will have to go,' Gina decided. She opened the cabinet and started to take out the pieces. 'OK, Sara. Let's start with this teaset.' She turned a saucer upside down. 'This is one for the auction room, I think.'

Garvie put his head round the door when they were almost finished.

'How many teacups did these people need? Unbelievable. Sweetheart, I've got to run down to Inverness. You don't need the car this afternoon, do you?'

Gina shook her head.

'I'm not going anywhere but, Rob, why do you need to go to Inverness?'

Garvie put his finger beside his nose.

'We do have our first wedding anniversary coming up, Mrs Hammond.'

Sara was looking at them both, puzzled.

'Are you wondering who Rob is?' Gina laughed, indicating her husband.

'There was another Robert Hammond already on the list when he started acting so he couldn't get an Equity card in his own name. He chose to call himself Garvie professionally. Now he's quite happy to answer to both, but it is confusing if you don't know.'

Sara looked at Garvie's slightly crinkly black hair and his bright blue eyes. He didn't look like a Robert to her.

'I think Garvie suits you. I can't think of you as anything else. Except Hardcastle, of course!'

'I left Mr Hardcastle back in London, Sara. Call me Garvie, call me Rob — call me Darling, if you like. I don't mind!' He stepped into the room, holding Toffee by the collar. 'I'll be back by dinner-time. I should have made my appointment for the morning — I forgot how long it takes to drive to Inverness.'

'Appointment? You're being very mysterious.' Gina raised her eyebrows at her husband, who looked as if he regretted that slipping out. He waggled his eyebrows in return but didn't volunteer any further information.

Letting go of the pup, Garvie came forward to say goodbye. Delighted to be unrestrained, Toffee capered towards the carefully stacked china.

As one, Garvie, Gina and Sara dived after her, catching her just before the big golden paws could do any damage.

Fire!

Sara was still laughing over the incident as she went up the road.

If only this job were for longer. It was fun being with the Hammonds and it was really satisfying making neat records for Gina, showing what she wanted to do with the contents of the Lodge.

Poking around in someone else's cupboards and nooks and crannies and getting paid for it — jobs didn't come much better than that. She would be very happy to stay in Farrshore if it was permanent.

But it would only take a couple of months at the most before the Lodge was cleared and ready for the next stage of renovation, a stage in which she wouldn't have a part.

She would sit down tonight and put her organisational skills to another use. She would draw up lists of pros and cons and look quite scientifically at which list was longer. Then she would go with that decision. Whatever it was.

She hadn't felt like eating breakfast and had refused Gina's offer of a sandwich so she would make lunch for herself and the children before taking them to the beach. She'd impressed upon Rosie that she was not to go treasure-hunting in caves again without an adult. Rosie had promised to stay in their back garden this morning and Tyler, looking slightly mutinous, Sara thought, had said he would stay, too.

With Dolly and Magnus nearby they would be quite safe.

'Sara.' Cathryn, standing with Thelma and Peter outside Dolly's house, waved her over. 'How's it going? Are you enjoying working at the Lodge?'

'I love it,' Sara said. 'I was just thinking how lucky I am to be there, even if it's just for a short time.' She told them what she was doing.

'Sounds a bit like archaeology.' Peter laughed. 'Rummaging about in the lives of people who are now history.'

'That's one way of looking at it,' Sara agreed. It was rather like that, and so was genealogy, now she came to think about it. It seemed easier to deal with the past than with the future.

Magnus opened the door.

'Having a party? Why wasn't I invited?'

'Sara was just telling us about the Lodge,' Cathryn said. 'Dolly says Garvie's offered to have the ceilidh so we'll all get a chance to see inside.'

'I don't think I'll — ' Thelma began. She put her hand behind her ear. 'Where on earth is all that noise coming from?'

Magnus sniffed.

'Do you smell smoke?'

'That's Rosie calling.' Sara started running. 'It's coming from our back garden.'

Round the corner of the house she stopped in horror.

Fire was licking under her fence and starting to spread up the hill, over the dry heather.

6

Fire!

Magnus and Peter raced after Sara, followed at a more sedate pace by Thelma.

Cathryn caught sight of JD and Dolly looking in surprise through the sitting-room window.

She dashed into the house.

'Whatever's the matter?' Dolly was standing behind JD's chair with her hand on his shoulder.

Cathryn didn't want to alarm them.

'I'm not sure. We heard shouting from Sara's back garden and smelled smoke.'

'Smoke!' JD made to rise from his chair, forgetting that he couldn't do that. He smacked the arm in frustration. 'Smoke! The ground's so dry, any fire will be up the hill in a minute. Will

170

Sara know where the brushes are?'

'I doubt it.' Dolly started pushing JD out of the room. 'Beating brushes,' she said to Cathryn, who was looking puzzled. 'If you catch a fire in time you can use them to stop it spreading. Yes, JD, I'm going as fast as I can.'

'Where are these brushes?' Cathryn asked, walking quickly beside them. 'I could go on ahead and get them.'

'About fifty yards up the hill. There's a kind of stand — there should be two brushes. We must stop it before it reaches the new tree plantation.'

'How in the world could it have started?' Dolly wondered, as Cathryn started running.

'Tell Sara to fill her sink and get her pots and pans out!' JD called after her.

Sara had evidently already thought of that. When Cathryn rounded the corner she saw Thelma and Sara and the children carrying various utensils filled with water from the back door to the end of the garden. Peter was trying to get a hosepipe attached to an outside tap and Magnus was on the other side of the fence beating the ground with what appeared to be an old sack.

The area of scorched earth was gradually getting bigger as the fire smouldered its way up the hill.

Cathryn climbed over the fence and grabbed Magnus by the arm.

'There are brushes,' she began. She looked up, scanning the hillside for the stand JD had told her about. 'Beating brushes. Look, up there.'

Fortunately Magnus seemed to grasp what she meant. He handed her the sack.

'I'll get them.' He bounded off up the hill.

Cathryn hit the ground with the sack, choking as the smoke and ash rose up.

Then Magnus was beside her, handing her a brush with a long handle. Together they began to keep the fire at bay. All Cathryn could see was the blackening ground as she beat and beat.

Eventually she stood up straight to stretch her back. Her hand was grimy but she ran it over her face anyway. Down in Sara's garden, other people seemed to have appeared, enough of them to form a couple of chain-gangs getting water to the fire as fast as they could. JD was in charge of the hose now. It was something he could do from his sitting position. It looked as if he was in the centre of it all — Cathryn could hear him urging the others on.

She started beating again. Magnus moved towards her as the fire snaked in her direction.

'Have you used these before?' Cathryn gasped out the question.

Magnus shook his head.

'But I've seen them being used.' He stamped his foot over a flame in a reckless fashion. 'A forest fire when I was a kid.' He must have rubbed his left eye with a hand as grubby as her own. It made him look as if he was winking at her.

She swallowed.

'How do you think it started?' Magnus pressed his lips together.

'I know how it started. And I shall be having a word with my son as soon as we're finished here.'

'You think Tyler . . . ' Cathryn began, as Peter came up, holding out his hand for her brush.

'I'll take a turn.'

Gratefully, Cathryn handed it over.

'We're winning,' Magnus said, clapping her on the shoulder. 'It's almost out.'

Cathryn headed down the hill and back into the garden.

'Well done, lass,' JD greeted her. 'It would have been a tragedy if it had reached the plantation. The old laird was determined to have native trees there and they're coming on nicely.'

Cathryn sank down on to the grass, suddenly feeling exhausted.

Team Effort

Dolly clapped her hands to get everyone's attention.

'I suggest we go to the hall for a cup of tea. Sara's teapot isn't big enough for all of you!'

Tyler dropped down beside Cathryn. 'Is Dad very angry with me?'

'Was it you, Tyler? What did you do?' Cathryn asked, trying to keep her voice low and sympathetic.

'Just showed Rosie how to make a fire without matches. We were going to toast marshmallows. I did make a circle of stones first but I guess it wasn't good enough.' His eyes filled with tears. 'There were sparks and then the grass started burning really quickly.'

'It's all out now,' Cathryn reassured him. 'Don't worry. Look, here's the fire brigade. They took their time.'

'Sara called them but the fire station is fifty miles away, JD says,' Tyler said, sniffing.

'Do you want this?' Cathryn asked, handing him a tissue from her pocket.

'Here's Dad.' Tyler stood up, squaring his shoulders. 'Boy, am I in trouble.'

Cathryn gave his arm a sympathetic

175

squeeze and left them to it.

In the hall, Thelma was putting out cups and Cathryn could see Dolly filling an urn in the kitchen.

JD's chair was in the middle of the floor. Rosie was perched on his knee and he was surrounded by the various neighbours who had come to help.

'A great team effort,' JD was saying. In contrast to Rosie, who was quiet for once, he seemed enervated by the whole episode. He'd proved, Cathryn thought, that he was just as good in a crisis now as when he was on his feet.

An Unexpected Visitor

Cathryn went to the ladies' room to wash her hands. Sara was already there. Her face was pale, eyes ringed with dark circles, like a panda's. She stood aside slightly so that Cathryn could get to the wash-hand basin, and their eyes met in the mirror. Two pandas!

Cathryn burst out laughing and after

a moment Sara joined in.

'Don't bother trying to wash your face. The water's cold and there's just that little bit of soap.'

Cathryn took her advice. She glanced over as she was drying her hands and noticed Sara, now she had stopped laughing, looked pinched and white. It must have been such a shock for her, finding the fire and knowing that Tyler and Rosie had something to do with it.

'There's no harm done,' Cathryn said encouragingly. 'Tyler's very upset. I don't think he'll go toasting marshmallows in the garden again.'

Sara sighed.

'I hope not. Or I can't leave Rosie with him — I'll have to start taking her down to the Lodge with me. I thought he was a sensible boy.'

'He *is* sensible.' Cathryn found herself defending Tyler. 'And he and Rosie seem to get on so well.'

'I know, I know. She'd have been lost without him this summer.'

'Maybe Garvie could find him

something to do around the Lodge,' Cathryn suggested.

'That's a thought. I'll ask him. Oh, guess what?' Sara let out a hoot of laughter. 'Apparently Garvie's real name is Robert. He changed it when he started acting.'

Cathryn laughed, too.

'Really? Well, Garvie suits him better, I think.' She glanced out of the little window. 'Talk of the devil. There's Garvie and Gina. And there's another car drawing up. It's like Piccadilly Circus here today, isn't . . . oh!'

'What's the matter?' Sara joined her at the window, looking curiously at the man who had just got out of the car.

'It's my ex-boyfriend! It's Daniel!'

* * *

'We heard the fire engine,' Garvie boomed round the hall. 'Is everything all right?'

Several people began to tell him

about the afternoon's events.

Sara could see Magnus and Tyler sitting at the side of the room, Magnus with his arm around his son. She started in their direction but Garvie got there before her, and sat on Tyler's other side.

'I hear you're good at making fires,' he said.

'I didn't mean it to spread,' Tyler said.

'These things happen.' Garvie's voice was much gentler than usual. 'Look, we're tidying up the Lodge, as you know. I was planning on having a bonfire or two. Do you want to come down and help me some time?'

Tyler looked at his father for guidance.

'Would you like to do that?' Magnus asked.

Tyler nodded.

'Excellent,' Garvie said. 'I could do with another man about the place.'

Tyler smiled, his teeth white in his dirty face.

Magnus took his arm from the boy's shoulders.

'Go get Rosie and play some basketball. I'll come over when I've finished my tea.

'That was good of you, Garvie.' He turned to the other man as Tyler ran off. 'Kids, eh? I feel as if I've aged ten years this afternoon.'

'Never had any myself, but I remember what it feels like to be one. All that energy. It has to go somewhere.'

Shock

Sara grabbed a cup of tea and sank into the vacated seat between the two men. Magnus looked at her.

'You OK, Sara?'

'I'm fine. Listen, Magnus, I've just had a thought.' She turned to smile at Garvie then put her hand on Magnus's arm. 'Garvie told me that he changed his name for professional reasons. And I wondered, what if your great-grandfather changed his name when he left here? That would explain why we can't find any trace of him.'

Magnus sat up straight.

'Sara, that's brilliant. New life, new name. It makes sense. So, Finlay Macaskill changed his name from — what? How can we find out?'

Sara looked over to where JD was still holding court. She felt excitement rise and put her hands over her mouth for a moment.

'Oh, Magnus, it could be that your great-grandfather was JD's great-uncle.'

'What? How do you work that out?'

Sara told him about JD looking up his family on the internet and finding his great-uncle John, middle name Finlay, born the same year as Magnus's great-grandfather, who had run away to sea. It all added up to them being one and the same person.

Magnus jumped to his feet.

'What will we do first, Sara? Go and check the records again? It's amazing! I must tell Cath.' He scanned the room.

'Where is she? Did she go back to Dolly's?'

'I don't know where she is now, but her friend Daniel just arrived. She went outside to see him.'

Magnus went over to the open door of the hall and looked out. Cathryn, in her grimy, scorch-marked summer trousers and T-shirt, had her back to them. Beyond her, a dark-haired young man in a suit was leaning against a very smart car. He was reaching out his hand to Cathryn's face.

Magnus stopped, turned around and went back into the hall.

* * *

As she left the hall, Cathryn's mind was whirling. Maybe it was reaction to the afternoon's events and the hard physical effort of beating back the fire. Or maybe it was the shock of seeing Daniel in the little car park outside the hall. What would she say to him? What would he say to her?

182

'Was that Garvie Hammond I just saw?' Daniel was looking over her shoulder. 'Garvie Hammond from 'Hardcastle'?'

'He's bought the big house at the bottom of the hill. It's nice to see you, too, Daniel.'

'Cathryn! Come here. I'm sorry. It was just so unexpected seeing him out of context, in the back end of nowhere.' He made to hug her but recoiled as he took in her appearance. 'What on earth have you been doing?'

'Oh, just a bit of fire-fighting. One of the things you find yourself doing in the back end of nowhere.'

Something in her tone made Daniel realise that he'd got off on the wrong foot.

'It's certainly beautiful here,' he said, trying to recover the situation. 'But what was on fire and why did you have to put it out?'

'It's a long story.' Cathryn saw herself reflected in the wing-mirror of Daniel's car. 'Sorry, I know I look a sight. How did you know I was here?'

'Why were you trying to hide from me?'

'It wasn't like that! You made it clear that our relationship was finished. I got the chance of coming up here for a few months and I took it. That's all.'

'You wouldn't let your friends tell me where you were.'

Cathryn held his gaze.

'Why did you want to know?'

'You just disappeared. So when I found myself in the West Country last week I went to see your parents. They said you were here, on secondment from the department for a dig.'

Cathryn couldn't be angry with her parents. They had no reason not to give Daniel the information.

The long weekend they had spent in Cornwall with her parents last autumn had been the first time they'd spent more than a few hours there together. It had been, Cathryn thought, a successful little holiday. Daniel had been warmly welcomed by Cathryn's mother and father, and by her sister, who lived with her family nearby, and he'd seemed to enjoy himself.

But only a short while later he had told Cathryn that he had met someone else.

Daniel reached out now and tucked a strand of her hair behind her ear. Then he was looking over her shoulder again.

'That's the bloke I met in London. Marcus something. The film producer.'

Cathryn looked round to see Magnus turning on his heel on the hall step and going inside. How long had he been standing there?

She took a step backwards.

'His name's Magnus. Daniel, have you come here to see Magnus or to see me?'

Daniel laughed, a little uneasily.

'What do you think? But we can't talk here. Can we go and find a café?'

Cathryn couldn't help laughing.

'There's no such thing in Farrshore. Anyway, I can't go anywhere looking like this. I'll go and wash and change. Do you want to wait in the car?'

'On you go. I'll have a mooch about. See what it is you like so much about this place. Your mother said you were quite taken with it.'

Cathryn was thinking furiously. For some reason she didn't like the thought of Daniel 'mooching about', maybe wandering into the hall. Talking to Magnus.

'Look, come over to Dolly's, where I'm staying — I won't take long.'

It seemed very odd letting herself into Dolly's with Daniel behind her. She parked him in the sitting room and ran upstairs.

After the quickest shower on record she tied back her wet hair and got changed. No time to think about what to wear. She grabbed what came nearest, a summer dress she hadn't worn here before, white with big blue flowers.

Daniel was at the bottom of the stairs.

'You look pretty.'

Cathryn almost pushed past him.

'I'm sorry, Cathryn. I know I hurt you. It was just, after Cornwall . . . '

He stopped.

'After Cornwall, what?' Cathryn turned to face him.

'Well, you know.' Daniel wouldn't meet her eye. 'Your parents happily married since the year dot, your sister talking about babies all the time — I felt as if everyone assumed that's what we wanted, too.'

'Why didn't you ask me what *I* wanted?'

'Maybe I didn't want to hear the answer.'

'Can we go and talk about it somewhere else?' Cathryn opened the door, feeling almost frantic that Daniel should leave before meeting any of her new friends. It just seemed wrong, him being here.

'Where?'

Cathryn ran the geography of the area through her head.

'There's a hotel about ten miles back down the hill. They probably do afternoon teas. We can go there.'

They walked across to the hall car park.

'You still haven't explained why you're here,' she said.

Daniel put his hand on her arm.

'I didn't realise how much I'd miss you. Can't we go back to how we were before?'

Her heart used to jump with joy when he looked at her like that, but now it stayed perfectly still.

They reached Daniel's car and he opened the passenger door.

Cathryn looked over the top of the car to the hall. Was that Magnus at the window?

'Look, to save you having to drive me back I think I'll take my own car. You can follow me down the hill.'

'But — '

Without stopping to listen to Daniel's expostulations Cathryn ran back across to Dolly's, where her car was parked at the side of the house. With her own transport she would be free to leave whenever she wanted, and Daniel could carry on driving south.

A Cosy Reunion

Magnus came back into the hall, feeling rather shaken. When Sara had told him that it was very likely his family roots were right here in Farrshore his first thought had been to share the news with Cathryn.

That night, when they had sat outside in Achbuie eating fish and chips and he had told her about Sara drawing a blank with her research, she had been really sympathetic and encouraging. Later, when they walked along the beach and she'd described her Viking comb and whom it might have belonged to, he'd taken heart.

If archaeologists could figure out how people lived more than a thousand years ago, even be able to name some of them, then finding a great-grandfather, born merely a hundred or so years earlier, should not be impossible.

How odd that Sara should have unlocked the mystery by thinking about Garvie Hammond and the name requirements of the acting profession. No, he couldn't wait to tell Cathryn all about it.

But maybe he would never get the chance. That looked like a cosy reunion between her and Mr Ear-ring out there. She might not be interested in Magnus Macaskill's search for his ancestors any more.

Sara, interrupting his thoughts, took his elbow and led him over to her father-in-law.

'I'm going home to look online to find out more about JD's great-uncle. Why don't you tell him what we suspect? He'll be thrilled to bits.'

'I hope we're right. Do you think we should wait until we're sure?'

'Go on. Ask him if he can remember anything else about John MacLeod. I'll be back as soon as I can.'

Magnus got one of the chairs set out

to dry a couple of weeks earlier. It was certainly dry now, the seat very stiff and dusty. But he was so dusty himself from the fire that he didn't bother to wipe it. He placed it in front of JD and sat astride it.

'Tyler all right?' JD asked. 'Hope you didn't give him a hard time. Boys will be boys. I could tell you a tale or two about when I was that age. I remember once my brother and I — '

'JD. Sorry to interrupt. I'd like to hear that story, but can I tell you something? You know your great-uncle John?'

JD looked startled.

'What about him?'

'Sara thinks, and I think too, that when he left here he ended up changing his name. Using his middle name and calling himself Finlay, Finlay Macaskill. And that he settled in Canada and was my great-grandfather.'

'Your great-grandfather! John MacLeod! Good heavens, Magnus. Then we're, we're — '

'Related. Yes, I hope so. I can't figure out what you are to me, though.'

JD reached out and shook Magnus's hand vigorously.

'Something or other once removed, I expect. It doesn't matter. I wish my father was still alive to hear this. John MacLeod was the youngest of his family. My father never met him, but his older sisters did. They told him they remembered the commotion when it was discovered that John had run away.'

'Did he leave a note?'

JD shook his head.

'He was working on the Farrshore estate, as it was then. It employed most of the men around here, including John's own father. John was to be a gamekeeper but his heart was never in it, apparently. He spent most of his time, time when he should have been working, at the fishing harbour at Achbuie.'

Magnus pictured the harbour he and Cathryn had looked out on from their picnic bench.

'One day he didn't come back,' JD went on. 'The word came from Achbuie that he'd signed up to go on a herring trawler.'

'And no-one heard from him again?'

This time JD nodded.

'That's all I know. But my father had the feeling that John had never had a good relationship with his father, and his mother was dead, so he just cut loose and, from what you say, forgot he was ever John MacLeod.'

'Do you know what he looked like?' Magnus couldn't see any resemblance between himself and the man sitting in front of him, part of his long-lost family.

'We've got no photos from as far back as that,' JD said regretfully.

'I'm pretty sure we don't, either, but I'll phone my dad tonight. He'll just be so thrilled.'

'Does he look like you?' JD scrutinised Magnus's face.

'Not really. He says I look more like his own father.'

'What are you two talking about?' Dolly came over to take JD's cup.

'I'll tell you later, Dolly, love. Something that will knock your socks off.'

Magnus stood up. He walked over to the window. Cathryn and Daniel were walking closely together into the car park. Daniel held his passenger door open.

'Magnus?'

He turned round. JD was beckoning him.

'I couldn't keep quiet. I've told Dolly.'

Dolly reached up and hugged Magnus.

'I can't believe it. It's lovely news. Fancy you staying in our house all these weeks and none of us knowing we were family.'

Magnus hugged her back.

'I couldn't have hoped to find a nicer family, Dolly. I'm going to go over to see if Sara's found out anything else.'

'I'll come with you.'

JD rolled himself over to the door

and Magnus went behind the chair to help him down the step.

The car park was empty.

Happy To Stay

Sara had just opened her door when she heard scampering on the path behind her. She turned round to see two little ragamuffins, apparently quite oblivious to what they looked like.

'Rosie, I'm going to run a bath for you. Tyler, I'd suggest you go home and have one too.'

'Aaaw, Mum! Tyler and me thought — you know Daddy's old tent, the one in the hall cupboard? We thought we could put it up in the garden to use as a den.'

What would these children think of next? Sara opened her mouth to say no, but changed her mind. She didn't have time to supervise Rosie's bath right now. She couldn't wait to get online and follow her hunch.

'Well, I suppose so. But it's an old-fashioned one — do you know how to put it up, Tyler?'

'I'll figure it out.'

She left them spreading the canvas on the grass and puzzling over ropes and pegs.

At her desk she drummed her fingers impatiently as she waited for the records she wanted to come up.

JD's great-uncle John was recorded in the census for 1901, living in Farrshore with his father.

She looked up his father's wedding certificate and there was the proof she was looking for.

Macaskill. The maiden name of John Finlay MacLeod's mother was Macaskill. That's where he'd got his new surname.

Sara sat back in her chair with her hands behind her head, savouring the moment. She felt like a detective who has just solved a case and it was a very good feeling.

Rosie came up behind her.

'Can you come and help us? Tyler's

all mixed up in the tent.'

Though she didn't know it, Rosie was talking about a boy who must be her fourth cousin. But it wasn't Sara's story to tell.

'I don't think I'd be much help. Listen, is that someone at the front door?'

Rosie ran to the window.

'Goody. It's Grandpa and Magnus. I'll let them in.'

Magnus looked at Sara over Rosie's head, his eyebrows raised.

Sara nodded, smiling.

'His mother's maiden name was Macaskill.'

Magnus hunkered down to speak to Rosie.

'Where's Tyler? Could you go and get him? We've got something to tell you.'

Rosie grabbed his hand.

'You come out to the garden.' She giggled. 'Tyler's tied up at the moment.'

'Joe's old tent,' Sara said in answer to JD's questioning look as Magnus allowed himself to be pulled through the house. 'JD, your great-uncle was still here in 1901. When do you think he ran away?'

'Not long after that, I would think,' JD said. 'My father was born in 1904 and he was gone by then. If there are lists of trawlermen he might be in there.'

One Of The Family

'Now I know his real name there are all sorts of places I can look to find out more,' Sara said happily. Her course tutor would be able to advise her about Canadian records.

But this was much more than just an assignment. This was about real people and she couldn't wait to have another ancestor to find.

The phone rang and as she picked it up she saw the red voicemail light flashing.

'Sara? I've just got a minute. Is everything all right? I've tried a couple of times — did you get my messages?'

'Joe! It's been an eventful afternoon here. Everything's fine now. Can we speak later when Rosie's in bed? I've got a lot to tell you. But, oh, Joe! I've found Magnus's ancestor and it turns out he's related to you, to the MacLeods.'

'Wow! That is something. Listen, love. One of the guys was saying there's a job going in your old firm. Do you want me to find out more?'

'What?' For a moment Sara wondered what on earth Joe was talking about. 'Oh, no. I don't think so. I'm enjoying the jobs I've got here.'

'I've got to go now. Sara, does that mean you're happy to stay?'

'Yes, Joe, I want to stay in Farrshore.' She smiled at JD as she hung up.

That was one piece of news he could go home and share with Dolly.

Staring Into Space

Magnus hit the last tent peg into place. 'There's your den. Go inside. I'm going to tell you a story.' He sat down, facing them. 'Sara has discovered that JD's family and our family, Tyler, are related. Old Finlay was JD's great-uncle. So that makes you and Rosie kind of cousins.'

'I always wanted a cousin.' Rosie's eyes were round with excitement. 'I didn't know it would be Tyler. So are you my uncle?'

'Er, no. I don't think so. Better ask your mom. She's the expert. Now, please, you two, stay out of mischief.'

Instead of going back into the house, he walked round to the front garden. Under the window there was a wooden bench Joe had made.

Magnus sat down, needing to clear his head. He didn't know what to think about first — 'Old Finlay' or Mr Ear-ring. Taking in a deep breath of tangy Farrshore air, he planned what he would say to his father tonight.

But it wasn't his father's face he was seeing in his mind. It was Cathryn's, as she gamely worked with the beating brushes on the hill, as she sat comforting Tyler after the fire was out. The first time they met, on the road that rainy night back in May.

Had she asked Daniel to come to Farrshore?

As he stared into space, Cathryn's car drew up. She opened her back door, emerging with what appeared to be Achbuie Highland Toffee wriggling in her arms.

Up the hill came another car, going rather fast. It stopped behind Cathryn's and Daniel got out.

'I thought we were going to talk.' He grabbed her arm. 'What do you think you're playing at?'

7

Runaway

People were beginning to leave the hall now, among them Garvie and Gina who stared in surprise at Cathryn and then at each other as they saw her carrying their precious pup.

As Magnus left Sara's garden and started to cross the road, Garvie and Gina hurried towards Toffee. Daniel stood beside Cathryn, his outburst halted by the appearance of the others.

'I thought you'd shut her in the kitchen,' Gina said.

'I thought *you* had. I should have checked. Where did you find her?' Garvie asked.

'She was standing wagging her tail at the end of your drive. Luckily she let me lift her up and put her in the car.' Cathryn handed the dog over.

She had got freshened up and changed into a summer dress, Magnus noticed. To look at her now you would never have guessed she'd had a gruelling afternoon. He must still be looking like a tar baby. He ran a hand over his chin. A shave as well as a shower would be a good idea. In contrast, Daniel was well-groomed, and sharply dressed in a suit and blue-and-white-striped shirt. He wasn't looking too happy, though.

'Can we go now, Cathryn?'

Magnus couldn't hear Cathryn's reply.

He had to pass the little group to get over to Dolly's and knew he couldn't avoid stopping to acknowledge them, but he really didn't want to. For one thing, he couldn't stand to see Cathryn and Daniel together. All he wanted to do was get washed and changed and phone Dad to tell him Finlay had been found. Then he wanted to sleep. For about a week.

Garvie hailed him.

'Look at our naughty little runaway.'

'Cathryn?' Daniel didn't bother to keep his voice down.

'You've done your good deed for the day. I've come all this way . . . '

'I didn't ask you to!' Cathryn's own voice became heated.

'We'll be off now,' Gina said tactfully. 'Take this rascal home. Thank you, Cathryn, for rescuing her.'

'I'm glad I was there at the right time.' Cathryn stroked the top of Toffee's head in farewell.

Now was the moment for Magnus to make his exit, too, but Daniel, it seemed, had just realised he was there and switched his attention from Cathryn.

Quite A Day

'It's Marcus Macaskill, isn't it? We met in London.'

'Magnus. Yes, in the lift. How did your meeting go?'

'Good. Good. Still waiting to hear something definite. These things seem to take for ever. So, what are you doing up here?'

Magnus looked at Cathryn and back to Daniel.

'It's still a bit hush-hush.'

'Has it got something to do with Cathryn being here?'

Magnus looked uncomfortable.

'I really can't say.'

'Daniel, please. Look, yes, we're here for the same reason but I can't tell you what that is.' Cathryn took a step away from him.

Daniel held up his hands in mock surrender.

'OK, OK. Now, let's go.'

Cathryn shook her head.

'I don't think we have anything to say to each other.'

Magnus started to walk away. This was definitely none of his business. Three was a crowd. And then there were four as Tyler ran up behind him.

'Dad! Are you going to be phoning

Grandad about Old Finlay? I want to speak to him, too.'

'Oh, what's happened? Has Sara found something?' Cathryn turned her head in their direction.

'Yes, and guess what, Cath?' It was Tyler who answered. 'Dad and me are related to JD and Dolly and Rosie.'

'What?' Cathryn moved near them. 'But how?'

'Well, Old Finlay was JD's uncle who ran away,' Tyler began, 'and he changed his name. He . . .'

Looking at Cathryn, her expression rapt as she listened to Tyler, Magnus suddenly felt sorry for Daniel. He was good-looking, clever, ambitious. But he wasn't the man for Cathryn Fenton.

'Hey, Daniel.' He could afford to be generous. 'I'm going to London next Monday for ten days before I go to Orkney to do some filming. Do you want to meet up? I've got some contacts who might be useful to you.'

'That's very good of you, Macaskill.' Daniel took out his wallet and extracted a card. 'My details,' he said. 'So, do you get back to London often? I imagine you miss it.'

'Not at all,' Magnus said.

'No? But this is just so . . . '

'So beautiful?'

'Well, yes. But so far away.'

'That's why I like it. Plus it reminds me of where I grew up — mountains, sea.'

'It's the city streets for me,' Daniel said. 'And that's where I must be getting back to now.'

There was a pause.

'I'll come with you to the car,' Cathryn said.

Magnus thought his son was behind him as he headed for Dolly's but Tyler had followed Cathryn.

'Gee, I like your car,' he was saying to Daniel as he prowled round the vehicle.

Daniel shrugged. Clearly, he'd given up trying to speak to Cathryn. He held her arms for a second and kissed her on the cheek. Then he was gone.

'It's been quite a day,' Cathryn said,

linking her arm through Tyler's.

Magnus could only agree.

★ ★ ★

'I really want to hear about your time in rep,' Gina said to Dolly as they chatted on the doorstep of the Lodge. 'Can you come in for a chat?'

'That would be lovely, if you're not busy. JD's watching the news programme but it seemed too nice an evening to stay inside, so I thought I'd pop down with your eggs.' Dolly followed Gina through to the kitchen. 'I've got a scrapbook at home with photos and press cuttings. Why don't you come up one morning for coffee and I'll show it to you? And I'd love to see your cuttings book some time.'

'Funnily enough, one did emerge from a box the other night,' Gina said. 'Do you miss it all, Dolly? The smell of the greasepaint . . . '

' . . . the roar of the crowd.' Dolly finished the quote. 'I don't recall much roaring in Pitlochry, but one whiff of greasepaint and I'm back there after more than thirty years.'

She sighed, then laughed at herself. Since Garvie had found out about her acting career she'd found herself thinking about it more and more.

It was funny. She'd picked up and dusted those pictures of herself in costume several times a week for years and years and never thought about them. Now, ever since Garvie had admired them, she looked at them often and long-forgotten lines of script came back to her. Not that she regretted for a moment her decision to marry JD when she had to choose between him and the rep, but — oh, what was the use of dwelling on the past?

'I Need Your Help'

Gina put a loose-leaf binder in front of her. 'This isn't a stage one, it's from when I was in the States three years ago.'

Dolly turned the pages with interest.

'Hollywood! I'd no idea you were in films as well as on the stage.'

'Just a couple of small parts but they made me offers I couldn't refuse and bought me the time I needed to have a break. I kept being ill — nothing very serious, but I felt below par. I've been acting professionally since I was nine, you know. I really wanted some time out. And when I came home, a mutual friend, with marvellous intuition, introduced me to Rob — to Garvie.'

'Do you think you'll make more films?' Dolly would have liked to ask more about Garvie. He and Gina made an unlikely couple in some ways.

'Never say never. But you get forgotten about quickly if you're not working. I'm not thinking about it at the moment. Garvie has another month before he must start on 'Hardcastle' again. I'm going to enjoy that time with him before I make any plans — well, that's not true.' She sat down beside Dolly. 'I did have a plan, an idea anyway. It's a long way from Hollywood. And I'd need your help.'

'Mine?' What on earth could Dolly MacLeod do to help Gina Hammond?

'Garvie and I went to a couple of events in the Achbuie Summer Festival and they were lovely, there was such a good atmosphere. But one thing the Festival doesn't have is any drama.' Gina put her hand over Dolly's. 'I thought you and I might start a drama festival to tie in with Achbuie, but using the hall here in Farrshore. We'll have to speak to the Achbuie people first, of course, but what do you think?'

'But the hall's not ready!' Dolly burst out. Her head was in a spin.

'We have a year,' Gina said. 'Garvie says some of his friends on 'Hardcastle' would be happy to contribute to any fund-raising. A few of them are planning to come up to the ceilidh. I thought we'd contact drama groups from all over Scotland and invite them to enter a competition. We can find adjudicators and a big name to present prizes.'

'But — ' Dolly began.

'It's maybe pushy of me, as a newcomer, to suggest it,' Gina said, taking her hand away.

'No!' Dolly was horrified that her hesitation was being misinterpreted. 'It sounds a wonderful idea, Gina. But I have no experience of running a festival.'

'I don't either. We can learn together. You're practical and you're warm and tactful, that's a great start.'

'Goodness.' Dolly was overcome. 'Well, you've made me an offer I can't refuse. I'd love to.'

'Brilliant.' Gina squeezed her arm and stood up. 'I think this calls for a celebratory glass of wine.'

Garvie put his head round the door as Gina took a bottle from the fridge.

'I take it she said yes?'

Gina got three glasses from a cupboard.

'This is the inaugural meeting of the Farrshore Drama Festival committee. Come and toast its success.'

'Of course it will be a success,' Garvie vowed. 'With you, my darling, and our lovely Dolly at the helm, how could it not?' He put his arms round Gina and gave her a smacking kiss. 'Didn't I say it was a cracker of an idea?'

Gina looked at him mischievously.

'Oh, it was your idea, was it?'

'Well, maybe a case of great minds thinking alike.' Garvie poured the wine. 'I'll take some of the credit. It was me who found out about Mrs MacLeod's racy theatrical past, after all.'

Dolly spluttered into laughter.

'I wouldn't put it that way.'

Gina raised her glass.

'Here's to our theatrical future. Let's put Farrshore on the map.'

Dolly could smell the greasepaint already.

Sara's News

Sara passed a box up to Gina who was perched on a ladder. Gina withdrew a length of tartan ribbon.

'What do you think, Sara?' she asked with a twinkle. 'Do you like what we're doing to the ballroom?'

'It will look just right,' Sara said diplomatically. 'All the tourists and Garvie's friends from London will think it's what a Highland ballroom should look like.'

'Good.' Gina looked around the room. 'Where is Garvie? He told me he was taking Toffee for a walk about half an hour ago.'

'I've just seen him in the garden talking on his mobile,' Sara replied.

'His mobile?' Gina repeated. 'He's been glued to that phone all morning. I don't know what he's up to. We could do with a hand here. There's such a lot to do before tonight.'

'Dolly and JD will be down soon to help.'

'Excellent,' Gina said. 'JD can keep Garvie in order, I hope. He's getting over-excited.' She laughed. 'Men are like small boys sometimes, aren't they?'

'I know Joe is, when he gets another boat to do up.' Sara smiled. 'What would you like me to do now?'

Gina looked down at her.

'Are you all right, Sara? You're looking pale.'

'I'm all right. It's just — can I talk to you for a minute?'

'Of course.' Gina came down the ladder, looking concerned. 'Shall I get you a glass of water?'

'No. Thank you. It's good news, actually. Joe and I are so thrilled. I'm going to have a baby in March.'

'Sara!' Gina went to fetch a chair from the side of the room. 'Sit down. That's fantastic.'

'I can hardly believe it,' Sara said. 'We've waited so long for a brother or sister for Rosie.'

'She must be over the moon.'

'She doesn't know yet. We've just told

JD and Dolly so far. We'll wait until Joe comes home — oh, that's something else to tell you. Anyway, Rosie's still getting over the excitement of finding a cousin and 'Uncle Magnus', as she's determined to call him.'

'Is Magnus still in Orkney, by the way?'

'He won't be here for the ceilidh, unfortunately. There was some kind of hitch in the filming and he can't get back in time. He phoned Cathryn this morning. She seemed really disappointed.'

'Yes, it's a shame. What were you going to tell me about Joe?'

Amazing

Sara took a deep breath. 'He's going to leave the rigs and come back to take up JD's business. So that's it. We're staying in Farrshore.'

'Well, I'm delighted to hear it,' Gina said. 'How do you feel about it? Quite sure?'

'Yes.' Sara nodded. 'It took me a long

time to feel at home here but I do now. I've got you to thank, Gina. Working here has been great — and being able to find Magnus's family. And now the baby. It will be lovely to have Joe at home all the time, and his mum and dad just across the road.'

'You don't have to thank me,' Gina said. 'I don't know what I'd have done without you.'

'Will you still need me to come down?' Sara asked, a little anxiously. She meant what she said about feeling settled in Farrshore, but working for Gina was part of the package, as it were.

'Of course. I'm so glad you want to,' Gina said. 'There's still a lot of sorting out to do. And later, if I go back to acting or if I'm in London with Garvie, I was wondering if you would be able to keep an eye on the Lodge?'

'No problem,' Sara said cheerfully.

'And you'll keep up the genealogy course, won't you? You know, I was thinking. There are a few family history centres around the country, aren't there? But there aren't any near here — and we've got all the estate records going back almost a hundred and fifty years. How would you feel about using those to start a centre here?'

Sara stared at her.

'Not now, of course,' Gina said hastily. 'You've got enough on your plate. But in the future.'

'You're amazing.' Sara couldn't help laughing. 'You've got Dolly running a drama festival and now this.'

'I'm good at talent spotting,' Gina said.

'Well, you spotted me.' Garvie had come up behind her and put his arms round her waist. 'Are we getting ready for a ceilidh night, ladies? Or are we just sitting around gossiping?'

'You can talk.' Gina twisted round to face him. 'Where have you been?'

Garvie avoided the question. He peered at Sara.

'Are you all right, Sara? You're a bit — '

'Pale. Yes, I know. I'm fine, thanks,

Garvie.' She stood up, exchanging smiles with Gina. 'There's JD and Dolly now,' she added as they appeared at the french window.

Garvie took his phone from his pocket.

'Catch up with you in a minute, JD. I need to make a call.'

Gina shook her head at him as he backed away.

'Garvie, what's going on?'

'There's a van coming down the drive,' JD announced as he wheeled himself through the door.

Garvie shot past the wheelchair and went outside.

He was back in a few minutes.

'It's the dance floor.'

'The dance floor?' Dolly queried.

'Yep, got it online. Hired. Bit of a problem getting one big enough. Had to send to Edinburgh for it. JD, maybe you could supervise here.'

'What are you going to do?' Gina asked, her eyebrows raised.

'That phone call,' Garvie said.

Gina shrugged and folded up the ladder.

'I'll finish this later, once the floor is down. Sara, Dolly, let's get out of the way.'

'There's another van,' Dolly said, looking out the window as Gina ushered them towards the kitchen.

'We certainly don't need to hire teacups — what with the ones from the hall and all the sets from here we could make tea for the five thousand tomorrow night!' Gina said. 'I put a load in the dishwasher earlier. Maybe we could store them in the little pantry and put another load on? That would be a big help. Sara, do you want to go home for a rest?'

'You've told Gina your happy news then?' Dolly said. 'I think that's a good idea, dear. Save your energy for later.'

'I think I will,' Sara said. 'I'll just go and say goodbye to Garvie and JD.'

She went back to the ballroom.

'I'm away. I'll see you — ' She stopped. Garvie was holding up a kilt against himself as JD lifted a black jacket from a box and smoothed it down.

'What do you think, Sara? I was worried it wouldn't arrive in time,' Garvie said. 'The driver got lost.'

Sara was speechless. That explained Garvie's furtive phone calls, maybe explained, too, the mysterious trip he'd made to Inverness a few weeks ago. Which meant that Gina knew nothing about it.

She went to stick her head round the kitchen door, grinning broadly.

'You'll never guess what arrived in the other van.'

Belle Of The Ball

'Ever done any Scottish dancing, Cathryn?' As if he were here asking her again, Cathryn could remember Magnus's question back at the beginning of the summer and squirmed a little as she remembered her reply: 'I didn't come here to dance.'

It had been true, of course, but she needn't have been so — how had Magnus described her to Peter? — starchy. She wondered if he still thought her that. She sighed. Well, now she was going to be dancing and Magnus wouldn't be there to see it.

'Cathryn?' It was Dolly knocking on her bedroom door.

'Dolly, you look lovely. That shade of blue really suits you.'

'Thank you, dear. What are you wearing?'

Cathryn held up an ankle-length dress in her favourite sea green.

'Is this too formal?'

'Not at all. It's gorgeous. You'll be the belle of the ball,' Dolly said admiringly. 'I came to tell you, Garvie's just rung to say they need another trestle table from the hall. Sara was going to drive to the Lodge anyway so that her car will be there for getting JD home later. So, as we're all dressed, JD and Tyler and I thought we'd just go down with her now. Is that all right?'

'Of course,' Cathryn said. 'What's the time? I'll see you in a little while.'

She spent some time on her make-up and on putting her fair hair up in a loose twist. The dress went on, and a pair of gold pumps. Dancing shoes. A green and gold wrap for the walk there and back.

In front of the house the road was deserted. A few raucous seagulls circled above her. Cathryn stood for a moment breathing in the salty evening air.

Viking Warrior

The seagulls were drowned out by a louder noise, and Cathryn looked up. A helicopter. A helicopter that looked as if it were about to land on the site. She gathered up her skirt in one hand so that she could run.

At the top of the path, she paused. The helicopter had landed in the field next to the site. Well, that was something. No harm done. Now she

223

felt silly, standing on the stony path in her long dress and flimsy shoes.

The blades came to a standstill and the pilot climbed down.

He took off his helmet and raised his hand in a familiar gesture to smooth his hair down. His hand remained in the air as he caught sight of her and the gesture turned into a wave. The evening sun glinted off his hair with its two sticking up horns, as he strode towards her.

Magnus Bare-Leg, the Viking warrior, was returning to Farrshore . . . although he'd chosen a different mode of transport this time.

Magnus caught hold of Cathryn's hand.

'You look like a tree, growing out of the path.'

A bubble of laughter broke from her.

'A tree?'

'A tree,' Magnus said firmly. 'With green leaves and golden blossom.'

He pulled her towards him and kissed her lightly.

'I thought you weren't going to be here tonight,' she said, trying to keep her voice calm, hoping it wouldn't betray the fact that her heart was jumping up and down.

'After I spoke to you this morning, after hearing your voice, I thought I must get to Farrshore tonight somehow.'

'By helicopter?'

'It's kind of far to swim, although I would if I had to. I knew the filming wouldn't be finished in time for me to get a ferry so I found a guy with a 'copter for hire.'

'You've got a pilot's licence?' Why was she talking when all she wanted was for him to kiss her again?

He nodded.

'Didn't know it would come in so useful. When does this ceilidh start, then?'

'Half past seven. Dolly and JD are there already, with Tyler.'

'I don't think Tyler was looking forward to it. Rosie was threatening to teach him to dance, the last I heard.'

Cathryn laughed.

'Rosie doesn't give up easily.'

'But Tyler's dad is looking forward to it, to dancing with you. Will you save the last dance for me, Cath?'

'Just the last one?' Happiness flooded over her.

'As many as you want. In fact, let's not go, let's just dance here under the sky.' He held out his arms. 'Will you — oh, hello, Thelma.'

Cathryn looked round.

Thelma was hurrying up the path. She stopped, as Cathryn had done, looking at the helicopter.

'I thought that contraption was landing on the site,' she said breathlessly. 'What's going on?'

There was a brief silence.

'Magnus came back for the ceilidh,' Cathryn said, feeling her face go pink.

'I see.' Thelma narrowed her eyes at Cathryn. 'Well. I'll walk back down with you now I know the site is all right. I'm looking forward to having the house to myself for the evening.'

226

'You haven't changed your mind about coming, then?' Cathryn asked as Thelma went in at her gate.

'Off you go. It's feet up and a good book for me. Oh, Cathryn?'

Cathryn turned, to catch Thelma winking at her. She glanced at Magnus to see if he'd noticed, but he was belatedly running his hand over his hair.

'It looks as if we're going, then.'

They followed a crowd of people and several cars down the drive to the Lodge.

Gina was at the door.

'Magnus, what a lovely surprise. If you're looking for Tyler,' she added with a smile, 'try the corridor behind the ballroom.'

* * *

Rosie linked her arm with Tyler's.

'Now we'll do Strip the Willow. We turn round and round . . . and . . . round.'

They whirled the length of the

corridor and back again.

'We need lots of other people to do that one properly. Let's do the Gay Gordons now. Put your arm like this.'

Magnus and Cathryn stood and watched Rosie pulling Tyler into position. Magnus put his arm around Cathryn's shoulders.

'Shall we have a go? A practice run would be a good idea.' He raised his voice. 'Rosie, can you teach us, too?'

Cathryn leaned against him for a moment, hearing the clamour of voices coming from the ballroom and wishing Thelma hadn't interrupted their private dance.

'Right,' Rosie said decisively, and Cathryn stood up straight. 'I'll dance with Uncle Magnus and Tyler will dance with Cathryn.' She grabbed Magnus's hand.

Gay Gordons

Tyler looked from his father to Cathryn as they moved apart, a question in his eyes. She felt her face flush for the second time that evening.

'I should warn you, Tyler,' she said, 'I've never done any Scottish dancing.'

Tyler looked at his watch.

'Ten minutes was enough for me.' He rolled his eyes to make Cathryn laugh.

'You'll like it better when there's music,' Rosie told him, and as if on cue the band began to warm up.

They moved through, Rosie still hanging on to Magnus.

Sara had described the ballroom to Cathryn. A long, wide room with a bulb swinging from the ceiling, a shabby carpet and dozens of deer antlers covering the walls. That was before its transformation for tonight. Sara reported that Gina had given in, laughing, to the décor Garvie had set his heart on.

The carpet was gone and a parquet dance floor installed. Wall-lights shaped like candles gave the room a gentle glow, and the Victorian atmosphere was added to by tartan ribbon bows adorning each and every antler. At one end of the room, on a little dais, was the ceilidh band.

Garvie came forward, holding up his hand for attention. His kilt, Cathryn could see, was the same tartan as the antler bows, and a white jabot spilled out from his jacket. She stifled a smile, remembering that Sara had told her Garvie had asked JD's advice about the purchase of his attire and sworn him to secrecy.

'Welcome to Farrshore Lodge,' Garvie said. 'Gina and I are very happy to see you. We're all here to raise money for the hall fund — and to have a good time. Enjoy the evening.' He turned to the band. 'Over to you, boys.'

'We'll begin with the Gay Gordons.' The bandleader lifted his accordion.

'Goody.' Rosie got into position beside Magnus.

He pulled her ponytail gently.

'I'll dance with Cathryn. But you must keep me a dance later on.'

'OK.' Rosie turned to look for Tyler

but he had sidled away to a table that held jugs of cold drinks for thirsty dancers. She chased after him.

Magnus moved towards Cathryn.

John MacLeod

'Good to see you, Magnus. Thought you weren't going to make it.' Garvie made his way towards them and cupped his hand under Magnus's elbow. 'Come through to my study. I've something to show you. Cathryn, perhaps you'd like to come, too?'

Cathryn followed as Garvie led the way to the back hall and into a small, untidy room, smelling faintly of tobacco.

'This was the old laird's office.'

He indicated the walls, crammed with black-and-white framed photographs.

'I've just got round to looking at all these properly. And what do you think I found?' Garvie lifted one off its hook.

'Look.' He pointed out the words *Farrshore Estate Workers 1900*. Underneath was a list of names. He handed the picture to Magnus.

'Say hello to your great-grandfather.'

Magnus ran his finger along the list and then up to the picture, Cathryn looking over his shoulder. Front row, third from the left. A tall young man wearing knickerbockers and a peaked hat. John MacLeod. His face was rather stiff and solemn like all the others posing for this official photograph, but there was no mistaking the resemblance to his great-grandson.

'I can't believe it. That's just amazing, Garvie. Has JD seen it?' Magnus asked, his voice choked.

'Showed him earlier. Told him I'd get some copies made for both of you. You can send one to your dad.'

'I wish I could be there when he sees it.' Magnus held out his hand to Garvie. 'Thank you.'

'Tyler will be interested to see it too,' Cathryn said.

'I'll bring him through here later, if I may, Garvie,' Magnus said. 'But first, Miss Fenton, we will have that dance.'

'In Love . . . '

A St Bernard's waltz was just being called and Magnus and Cathryn slid into place behind Dolly and Peter.

'Don't follow me, I haven't a clue what to do,' Peter told them, grinning. Dolly pointed out the 'caller', there to guide the uninitiated through the steps.

Magnus ignored the instructions and wrapped his arms around Cathryn.

'Alone at last. Almost.' His arms tightened. 'Cath. I've fallen in love with you. It kind of crept up on me for weeks and hit me on the head the night you found the kids on the beach. Any chance you feel the same?'

She raised her head to look at him. His blue eyes were soft and serious.

'Cathryn.' It was Dolly urging her forward to dance with Peter.

233

Cathryn was bewildered.

'It's a progressive waltz. You change partners.'

She hoped that Magnus could read her reply in her eyes, as she moved away to dance her way round the room.

For her, she thought, it had been the time they ate fish and chips by the harbour and talked into the long Scottish summer evening. Or maybe it was right at the beginning, that rainy night she stopped on the road to Farrshore to give a stranger a lift, and found a real live Viking.

Yes, she would tell him, she felt exactly the same.

THE END